"You had to know your business would raise eyebrows. It's unusual."

"Are llama treks a suspicious activity, Sheriff?" Samantha shot him a command-the-room smile.

Garrett found himself unaccountably taken aback by her direct gaze. "You…need to understand I'm talking to you as a father. I'd check out any situation I let my son into."

"So you want to know what kind of employer I am?" Her tone was pseudolight with a defensiveness that swam just below the surface. Her body language said he wasn't intimidating her.

He got the feeling this woman could hold her own. Anywhere.

Dear Reader,

Sometimes our identity is defined by external circumstances even as our heart tells us we are someone else altogether. Then what? What does it cost us to pick up and move on? My heroine, Samantha, must find the courage to begin a journey of change and self-discovery—oh, so much more easily said than done. Even as she thinks simplicity and solitude are the answer, she is wise enough along the way to accept the help of others at the same time that she reaches out to help. Subsequently, she finds the road less bumpy when traveled with valued companions.

And my hero, Garrett? He thinks he knows who he is and where his path should lead. But in reality, he's taken a safe and smooth route so that his world isn't rocked any more than it has been. Of course, Samantha—and love—are going to cause a much-needed detour!

Journeys. Sometimes it's better to ditch the road map and wing it, always open to the possibilities!

Enjoy!

Amy Frazier

SINGLE-DAD SHERIFF
Amy Frazier

TORONTO • NEW YORK • LONDON
AMSTERDAM • PARIS • SYDNEY • HAMBURG
STOCKHOLM • ATHENS • TOKYO • MILAN • MADRID
PRAGUE • WARSAW • BUDAPEST • AUCKLAND

ISBN-13: 978-0-373-71473-5
ISBN-10: 0-373-71473-4

SINGLE-DAD SHERIFF

www.eHarlequin.com

Printed in U.S.A.

ABOUT THE AUTHOR

Having worked at various times as a teacher, a media specialist, a professional storyteller and a freelance artist, Amy Frazier now writes full-time. She lives in Georgia with her husband, two philosophical cats and one very rascally terrier-mix dog.

Books by Amy Frazier

HARLEQUIN SUPERROMANCE
1269–THE TRICK TO GETTING A MOM
1298–INDEPENDENCE DAY
1423–BLAME IT ON THE DOG
1456–COMFORT AND JOY

SILHOUETTE SPECIAL EDITION
 954–THE SECRET BABY
1030–NEW BRIDE IN TOWN
1036–WAITING AT THE ALTAR
1043–A GOOD GROOM IS HARD TO FIND
1188–BABY STARTS THE WEDDING MARCH
1270–CELEBRATE THE CHILD
1354–A BUNDLE OF MIRACLES

Don't miss any of our special offers. Write to us at the following address for information on our newest releases.

Harlequin Reader Service
U.S.: 3010 Walden Ave., P.O. Box 1325, Buffalo, NY 14269
Canadian: P.O. Box 609, Fort Erie, Ont. L2A 5X3

CHAPTER ONE

GARRETT MCQUIRE LEANED ON the fresh timber and wire fence—erected properly within the surveyors' stakes, he noted—and looked out over the newly created pasture that had Tanner Harris in such a lather. As elected sheriff of Colum County, Garrett felt an obligation to listen to the concerns of all the citizens, but Tanner had been a sneak and a whiner all his life, someone who thought the world owed him, and he wore on Garrett's last nerve.

"When I saw you stop at the head of her road," Tanner said, "I thought you were gonna talk to her. Why didn't ya?"

Garrett took his time answering. Officially he was responding to Tanner's complaint against his neighbor's new fence. As sheriff, he didn't need to get into the fact his son was applying for a job at Whistling Meadows. To Tanner, that alone might look as if Garrett were taking sides. He wasn't. He hadn't even met the other side. Samantha Weston.

Although he'd seen her bicycling around town. Unless she broke the law—or messed with his son in any way—she was no concern of his. Maybe that's how he should approach the issue with Tanner.

"I didn't talk to her," he replied at last, "because she's done nothing wrong. Nothing I can see."

"Not technically, maybe." Tanner glowered at the offending railing. "But she's gone against time-honored tradition. Sashaying into town from who-knows-where. Buyin' up my family land. Cuttin' off access…"

Garrett tuned the guy out. He and the rest of Applegate's residents had heard this rant for weeks. In the barbershop. In the diner. At town meetings, even. And although the beef wasn't new, it had nothing to do with time-honored tradition—as much as boundary disputes came close to ritual in Colum County. Tanner's gripes all boiled down to the fact that his aging uncle Red had had the audacity to sell his sixty acres to an outsider rather than will it to his nephew. Three-quarters of Tanner's collateral had always been his presumed inheritance.

As to the comment that Ms. Weston had sashayed into town, she hadn't. She'd arrived and set up her business so quietly that, if it weren't for the new fence enclosing the pasture part of her property and the signs around the county, advertising llama day treks, you wouldn't think much had changed.

"…and the old man's makin' a fool of himself." Tanner had wound himself even tighter, if that were possible. "Living with her. A woman half his age."

"I don't think you can call it 'living with her.' You're ignoring the fact he sold her the land with the stipulation he can live out his days in the bunkhouse. Separate from the big house. On land he loves. Farmers don't usually get such a secure retirement. In cutting himself a creative deal, your uncle was thinking of his future."

"Well, he sure wasn't thinking of the future of his only kin. Me. With three boys to raise."

"No," Garrett replied, struck anew by Tanner's unrelenting self-centered attitude. "I dare say he wasn't."

Tanner grunted and seemed to be thinking along a different tack. "Between the national park and this fence, I'm blocked in. So where are me and my boys gonna ride our ATVs?"

"Rig yourself a trailer and haul your ATVs to the authorized county trails like most of the other folks around here. Your free-range days are over. Times are changing."

"Doesn't mean I have to like it." Tanner glowered at the top of the Whistling Meadows barn just visible above the far rise. "So, you're not gonna talk to her?"

"As things stand, I have no reason to." Garrett headed for his cruiser. "But I suggest you do. Neighbor to neighbor. Friendly-like."

"When hell freezes over." With a dismissive wave of his hand, Tanner headed across his littered yard toward his run-down house, which had been built too close to the boundary line as if in anticipation of the merging of the two properties.

Garrett got in his cruiser and glanced at his watch. Rory's interview with the Weston woman should be over by now. He hoped his son got the job. As soon as he'd arrived for the summer, the twelve-year-old had found the ad in the paper and had made the call himself. The only thing he'd asked his father for was a ride this morning. And although Garrett was glad Rory was showing some initiative, he wished he knew more of what was going through his son's mind these days. From the last visit to this, the preteen had closed down. Already reduced to seeing him on vacations, Garrett didn't like feeling further shut out of his only child's life. But if there was one thing he'd learned from experience with other people's kids, it was that you didn't find out much by pushing. Patience and observation were key—virtues easier executed in his job than in the role of parent.

PERCY TAGGING ALONG BEHIND, Samantha walked Rory McQuire toward the five other llamas wading in the creek. The boy had said very little, but he'd made eye contact as he'd listened to her explain the duties of the part-time job. And he'd let Percy make the first moves. He seemed easier around the animal than he was with her.

"Have you had any experience with llamas?" she asked.

"No, but I've read about them and most other animals. I watch the Discovery Channel. Animal Planet. National Geographic. I want to be a vet."

"How old are you?"

He patted his pocket. "I have my work permit." A work permit meant he was young. Standing on the bank of the stream, he watched Percy join his pack-mates. "Besides, does it matter? I'm strong."

"No, I guess it doesn't matter. I was just curious." She didn't like people snooping, either, and turned the conversation in a different direction. "Thinking how long I might expect your services before you head off to vet school."

He suddenly seemed uncomfortable, so she switched the subject away from him and onto her operation. "My herd's small right now because I'm just starting out. Besides, day treks with six llamas and a dozen or so paying customers are all I can handle by myself." And for the time being, at least, she needed to remain alone.

"Why aren't you out on the trail today?" he asked.

"Monday's our day off," she replied. "Not that

the boys need it. But if I don't take a break, work around the house and the property piles up. That's where you'd come in."

"Did you ever think of breeding? Seems like it would bring in more money than trekking."

She didn't care about the money. In fact, a small, obscure operation was just what the doctor had ordered. She'd experienced the personal pitfalls of a big enterprise. But she wondered why a kid who looked like he was in middle school cared about business.

"What made you think of the moneymaking aspect?"

"My mom's in banking," he replied with a shrug. "I can't avoid the subject."

"To answer your question," she said, strangely at ease talking to this kid as if he were much older, "I think I'll stick to trekking. Adding females to a herd leads to a whole other set of challenges. They're not particularly willing pack animals, and they can be moody."

Rory seemed to be taking mental notes. "How come you advertised for stable help," he asked at last, "when you said the llamas rarely go into the barn?"

"Force of habit. I grew up with horses. Even though the llamas stay for the most part in the pasture, the barn's full of tack and trekking equipment, and you'd be helping keep that in order."

Led by Percy, the five other animals had begun to drift over to the creek bank where the humans stood. Curiosity. Cats had nothing on llamas. Rory stood still. Not nervous, but waiting. Exuding a calm energy that, too, belied his years.

The three other kids who'd come seeking the job had been either too talkative or too boisterous in their movements or too touchy-feely. Llamas, like people, didn't wish to feel assaulted and, as cuddly as they appeared, didn't particularly like being snuggled or petted. They, more than she, had decided to pass on those first candidates.

She pointed to each llama in turn. "That's Percy. You already met him. He's what's called a paint. Then there's Mephisto, the bay. And Fred, the piebald. Mr. Jinx is an Appaloosa. The white one's Ace. And finally Humvee, the black and tan."

"Their coats are so different they're easy to tell apart."

"You'll learn you can recognize them as easily by personality."

Percy chose that moment to lean close and snuffle Rory on the neck. His muzzle, dripping with mountain creek water, must have been cold, but the kid stood his ground, merely chuckling. "What's he doing?"

"He's saying, 'You're hired.'"

"For real?"

"For real. Percy's chairman of my interview committee. Can you start today?"

"I'll have to ask my dad when he comes back."

"Of course." She hadn't paid attention to how Rory had managed to get to her farm. He'd simply shown up in her barn at the agreed-upon time as she'd been cleaning tack.

"He shouldn't mind if you could, maybe, give me a ride home when I'm done."

She tried to hide the reflexive wince. "Sorry. I don't drive."

Rory shot her a disbelieving look, but she was spared an explanation by the staccato double toot of a car horn. Partway down the hill, a cruiser had pulled up in front of the barn. The driver's door opened, and the sheriff got out.

"That's my dad," Rory said, heading downhill. "I'll tell him you want me to start now. I can walk home. I've walked farther. Other days I can ride my bike."

She didn't really want to meet the sheriff—she didn't need her second chance at life beginning with a connection to law enforcement—but, as an employer, she should say hello to this kid's father. So she set her shoulders and marched down the hill.

The boy and the man approached each other as if they weren't entirely at ease. After exchanging a few words, which Samantha couldn't hear, Rory came back up to her, dejection written on his features.

He looked at the ground as he spoke. "I can start today, but…I didn't tell you everything. Maybe you won't want me for the job."

"Try me."

He looked back at his father, who remained by the cruiser. "I'm only here for the summer. In September I go back with my mom. To Charlotte. Unless…."

"Unless?"

"Let's just say I can only promise you two months. The ad didn't say it was a summer job."

Percy felt comfortable with this kid. And so did she. Besides, two months to a person who was learning to live one day at a time seemed like forever. "Two months will be fine."

"You mean it?"

"Sure. But years from now I might ask you for a vet discount. Who knows?"

His only answer was a heart-melting grin.

"Come on. Introduce me to your father."

She told herself she had no reason to be nervous. Her business permits were in order. She hadn't sat behind the wheel of a car since her license had been revoked. She regularly attended her court-ordered AA meetings. Although her name change hadn't been sanctioned by the judge, she was Samantha

Weston only in Colum County. For personal reasons. All her business transactions bore the corporation name she'd established three months ago. A holdover reflex from her former life. Perhaps this bit of hedging meant she hadn't really disowned her past. She was glad Percy wasn't around to give her that soul-searching llama look.

"Garrett McQuire. Rory's dad." The sheriff held out his hand. He was tall and fit. Muscles were evident beneath a well-pressed uniform. Not much else showed, though. His facial features were well concealed beneath a Stetson and behind aviator sunglasses. Stereotypical, sure. But arresting.

"Samantha Weston." She tried not to be tentative in her handshake. "I run this place."

"She says I can work the summer." Rory still looked pleased, but a note of defensiveness had crept into his voice. Did the sheriff run his family the way he ran his department? "Maybe I could fill in other vacations, too, if Mom knows I'd be making money."

"You'll have to work that out with your mother, son. And Ms. Weston, of course."

Samantha didn't want to get into the middle of a custody mess. "Let's see how the next few days work out," she said. "You may change your mind. The work I need done isn't particularly glamorous."

"But the llamas are cool, Dad. You gotta meet 'em."

"Another time, okay? Now I'm due at the court-house. I'll be late tonight, too. Geneva will have your supper ready for you. She can stay if you want to play cards or video games."

"I don't need a babysitter," Rory mumbled.

"I know you don't. But you might want company." He turned to Samantha. All business. "Good to meet you. And welcome to Applegate."

Rory seemed relieved when it was just the two of them again. "What should I do first?"

"Let's go meet Mr. Harris. He used to own this land, and now lives in the bunkhouse. Although he doesn't work anymore, he still supervises."

Rory grinned. "Gotcha. Kinda like Geneva. She doesn't babysit. She supervises."

Red Harris, crafting fishing lures, was sitting in a rocking chair on the bunkhouse porch as they climbed the steep and rocky hill. "This here the new help?"

"You don't miss much," Samantha replied. "Mr. Harris, this is Rory McQuire."

Rory stuck out his hand.

The old man took it and hung on. "Now's a good time to get something straight." He looked directly at Samantha. "I'm not Mr. Harris. I'm Red. And since you, missy, are young enough to be my granddaugh-ter, and you, kid, could be my great-grandson, I sure would appreciate it if we all stuck to first names. Red, Sam and Rory okay with you two?"

Both Samantha and Rory, a little taken aback, nodded as Red shook Rory's hand forcefully. "You any good makin' lures?"

"Mr. Harris…Red." Samantha felt the need for a preemptive strike. "I hired Rory to do cleanup around the property. Maybe minor repairs. To help with the tack and equipment—"

"Just kiddin'," Red cut in with a wink to Rory. "If I had help with my lures, I'd get done twice as fast. Then what excuse would I have to sit on the porch and see how a city slicker runs a hardscrabble farm?" He chortled, and Samantha wondered at his assessment of her. She hadn't mentioned to him where she'd come from. "Let me tell you, kid," he continued, "weird animals or no, she's doin' a helluva lot better than my good-for-nothin' nephew woulda, had he got his greedy mitts on the property."

As Samantha resisted the point-of-pride urge to tell Red she'd grown up feeling far more comfortable in her father's stables and pastures than at her mother's posh parties, her BlackBerry vibrated. The caller ID told her it was her mom.

"I have to take this," she said to Rory. "You can start by clearing the tree branches from the paddock." The tumultuous winds of a thunderstorm last night had strewn her property with debris. "I'll be with you in a minute."

As she walked away, she heard Red say to Rory, "I might have to come up with a new name for her. She really isn't a Sam. Not at all. More like a Duchess..."

"Mother," she said quietly into the phone.

"Darling, how are you?" Her mother's concern was, and always had been, genuine.

"I'm wonderful." It was becoming the truth.

"Then, perhaps, your father and I could visit—"

"Please, we all agreed with Dr. Kumar. I need a total change. A year off."

"From us as well?" Her mother's voice held hurt.

"From everything."

"You know, dear, we're not the enemy."

"I know that. But my old habits are. I need time to forge new ones. Healthy ones."

"In secret?"

"Not secret. Seclusion."

"But why?"

"Because I'm vulnerable right now. And you know Dad. A steamroller in a tux." She smiled at the thought of the man she loved with an only child's devotion. "If I saw him, I'd be persuaded right back into the rat race."

"May I remind you Ashley International Hotels is a five-star rat race?"

"You know what I mean."

"And…now that we've broached the subject… will you be attending the opening of the Singapore Ashley? You worked so hard to get it up and running."

Samantha didn't quite know how to answer. Although she and her father had worked side by side on the project, although she knew it was his way of introducing her to the world as his heir in the luxury hotel corporation he'd grown from a small chain of economy lodges, she wouldn't be in Singapore for this event. Her heart wasn't in it. For her father's sake, she wished it were. But no matter that she had been immersed in the business from an early age and that her father implicitly believed in her—she wasn't a hotelier. Because she'd almost self-destructed trying to be someone she wasn't, she needed to find out who she might be.

"I did my job," she replied cautiously, "so that others could take over. And they will. Beautifully. With you and Dad there it will be a gala opening."

"Of course it will, but we'll miss you, darling. We do miss you. We only want you to be happy."

"Thank you. I'm working on it."

"Justin wants to know if he can call you."

"No." Justin Steele was her ex-almost-fiancé. She'd come to think of him as the fox in the henhouse. "When he proposed, I was very clear we had no future together."

"Oh, darling, that was the stress talking."

No. Of all the things she'd done to please others, turning down Justin had been the first genuine action she'd taken for herself. She wouldn't debate her mother on the issue.

After a long silence, her mother tried a different approach. "Can you give me a tiny hint as to where you are?"

"Mother!" As much as she missed her parents, Samantha needed this time. Alone. She didn't need her mother's well-intentioned meddling. And she certainly didn't need the intrusion of the paparazzi that had followed her arrest and court date. "I'm counting on you to honor Dr. Kumar's advice, and to make sure Dad doesn't send Max out on the trail." Max was the personal detective her father kept on retainer.

"You flatter me. I have very little real control over your father. As you say, a steamroller in a tux."

"I'm not trying to hide from you, Mother. Every day I feel stronger and stronger. But before I come home, I want to make certain I'm strong enough to avoid a repeat of—"

"An unfortunate incident. There's no need to bring it up."

"But part of my recovery is accepting responsibility."

"Darling, you had a drink or two during a social occasion. We all do. No matter what the judge thought, you are not a drunk."

"An alcoholic. A recovering alcoholic. And, over time, it was more than a couple drinks. In fact, so many drinks at that particular luncheon I don't even remember the school zone—"

"No!" The single syllable pierced the distance between mother and daughter. "You paid your debt. Can we, please, not relive it all?" her mother pleaded.

"Agreed. I'd like to focus on the present. And right now the sky is blue, the sun is shining and I'm breathing the most wonderful fresh air."

"Sea air? The Hamptons, perhaps? That lovely spa on the far end—?"

"Mother, you're incorrigible."

"Well, Dr. Kumar may have prescribed a year's rest, but you're not going to keep the location secret for the whole time, are you?"

"No. I just need to settle in." It had been three months since her rather secret—to keep the newshounds away—release from rehab. At first she hadn't wanted her parents to know her new location because she was afraid of being drawn back into her old life. Now, she was head over heels in love with the simplicity and beauty of Applegate, tucked away in the North Carolina Blue Ridge Mountains. Now, she was afraid if her parents showed up in town, they'd love it, too. So much so that her father would buy it and turn it all into a five-star resort.

LATER THAT NIGHT, GARRETT returned home, glad that today on the job had been routine. It wasn't always so. When he'd become sheriff five years ago, he'd inherited a mess. Colum County was changing rapidly. Developers were buying up mountain tracts and turning once nearly communal land into gated vacation communities and upscale commuter subdivisions, shutting long-term residents out and making their taxes stratospherically high. That was a minor intrusion compared to the influx of big-city problems. Drugs especially. Recreational drugs had replaced moonshine. The county remained a bucolic paradise on the surface, but underneath simmered some very real issues.

Sheriff Easley, his predecessor, had run things as his daddy and granddaddy had done before him—by a slow and convoluted good-ol'-boy system that didn't want to recognize change. The small department had been low-tech, ill-equipped and badly trained. Not to mention susceptible to the lure of small-town graft. A real embarrassment. Elected on a reform platform, Garrett had been vigilant in turning things around and confronting the county's problems head-on. Which meant he appreciated a routine day. A relatively quiet day. Like today.

He found Geneva in the kitchen, scrubbing a scorched pan. The smell of burnt popcorn filled the air. "How's it going?" he asked his housekeeper.

"It's going, all right," Geneva muttered as she lifted the pan and made as if to throw it out the window over the sink. "That boy uses my best pot to make popcorn. Puts in the oil then walks away to check on a video game. Smelling something not right, I come back here to find flames shooting out. My best," she repeated dourly. "Nearly ruined."

"I'll speak to him."

As Garrett turned toward Rory's room, Geneva caught his arm. "Don't." Her voice immediately changed from irritated to concerned. "He's been wrestling with something heavy. Been on that skinny little phone of his most of the evening with his mama. Won't tell me what's got him so riled." She returned to her scrubbing. "So don't mention this stupid old pot."

"I won't." He headed for a chat with his son.

In the three years since he and his ex-wife, Noelle, had divorced, Rory had spent every vacation with Garrett. It was part of the custody settlement. Garrett always looked forward to the return to day-to-day parenting, and Rory seemed to enjoy his time in the mountains, but the initial transition was always hard. This time especially so. At twelve, almost thirteen, Rory, with one foot in childhood and the other in adulthood, had stopped communicating with his father. It made Garrett worry his son might be getting ready to tell him he was too big for life in a small town and wanted to live full-time in Charlotte.

He knocked on Rory's bedroom door.

"Yeah."

Taking that monosyllable for permission to enter, Garrett pushed the door open. Rory was at his computer, intent on a game Garrett had seen his deputies playing. He didn't think it was appropriate for a twelve-year-old, but he needed to pick his battles. Right now he wanted to find out what was bugging his son.

"How did work go?" he asked. Up at Whistling Meadows Rory had seemed almost happy.

"Okay." His boy continued to play.

Garrett sat on the edge of the bed, facing Rory. "I'd like to talk."

Reluctantly Rory shut off the game, but he didn't face his father. Didn't speak.

"Geneva says you seemed upset."

Rory scowled as if fighting back tears, as if struggling to put the boy behind him.

"Son, I can help—"

"No you can't!" Rory twisted away. "Mom's made up her mind."

"About what?" Foreboding stabbed him. Despite their cool but cordial relationship so far, Noelle didn't reveal much about Rory's and her life in Charlotte, only her rise in the banking world. That was something she never tired of telling him, her proof, perhaps, that she'd been right and he'd been wrong about the limitations of Applegate. Now, what was going on? Was she thinking of remarrying? Or—the awful possibility hit him—was she tired of fitting Rory's trips to Applegate into her increasingly hectic schedule? Was she planning to seek sole custody? With her continued climb up the corporate ladder, she had the contacts and the financial wherewithal.

"What has your mother decided?" he repeated.

Rory whirled on the computer stool to face Garrett. Tears glistened in his eyes. He looked five, not twelve. "Mom wants to send me to boarding school after eighth grade."

Damn. This was out of left field. "Why?" His kid was bright and conscientious. Perhaps, at times, too conscientious. Too buttoned down. If Noelle had a fault, it was that she tried to make Rory a little pin-striped banker. "You're doing great right where you are."

"Mom says Harpswell Prep can help me get into an Ivy League college. But I wanna be a vet, and there are good vet schools that don't look at whether you went to some snooty high school or not."

Garrett felt the anger rise. Not at the notion of a prep school, but at the idea that Noelle had failed to consult him on a big decision in his son's life. And what a decision. She had to know it pushed his buttons. He hadn't spent his youth in foster care just so his son, with two loving parents, could get farmed out to boarding school.

"I'll talk to your mom," he said, rising.

"You can't talk to her now. She's on a plane to London. Besides, we need a plan, and I've been working on one."

Surprised, Garrett turned to his son. "What plan?"

"I want to live with you. Full-time. I don't want to go back to Charlotte. Mom's always traveling, anyway. We could switch the schedule. I could see her on vacations."

"Have you mentioned this to your mother?"

Rory shook his head.

Garrett could see the fireworks now. Noelle would think this was his idea. Would think he was using Rory to question her parenting skills, to circumvent the judge's orders. While she'd use all her considerable money and influence to make

Garrett pay, Rory would be the one to suffer in
the end.

Garrett couldn't let that happen.

CHAPTER TWO

"YOU LOOK LIKE THE WRATH OF God." That's what Geneva had told Garrett as she'd bustled through the kitchen door earlier that morning. Then, while getting eggs and bacon out of the refrigerator, she'd muttered, "I wouldn't worry so much if I thought there was a chance you'd been out on the town. Goin' a little wild. Havin' a little fun..."

She knew him better than that.

Last night, after leaving a message on Noelle's voice mail to contact him as soon as she arrived in London, he'd lain awake for hours, worrying the untold consequences of both her and Rory's separate plans. Not having heard from her by morning, he'd called her assistant in Charlotte, who had her itinerary. Overseas, Noelle was already in a closed meeting. Garrett needed to understand the time difference was five hours. Was it an emergency? If not, try Noelle again around nine, North Carolina time. She should have a small break before heading into another meeting, the assistant had said, promising to leave a message as well—

"Dad, look at that!" Rory said with disgust. Garrett had thrown the old banana-seat bike in the cruiser's trunk and was giving his son a ride to Whistling Meadows. "Someone's tossed garbage into the pasture. I'm gonna have to take care of that first thing. Before Percy and the boys eat something they shouldn't."

It made Garrett proud that his son was already taking ownership of this new job.

As they pulled up the farm road, Garrett could see six llamas haltered and tethered to the paddock fence. One carried a double-sided pack, and Samantha was adjusting another on a second animal. Four more packs lay on the ground. The llamas looked cool, calm and collected, but the woman looked frazzled.

Rory barely waited for the car to come to a stop before he hopped out. "Need help?"

"Yes, please!" Samantha moved from one side of the black-and-tan animal to the other, apparently trying to balance the contents of the bags. "Twelve Rockbrook campers and their counselor are booked for this morning. I just got a call they'd penciled in the time one hour earlier than I had. They're on their way. I'm not ready."

Garrett, noting she looked like a woman who preferred being in charge and prepared, stepped forward to pick one of the packs off the ground. "The cinch work looks simple. Anything in particular I should know?"

"The process is pretty straightforward," she replied, swiping wisps of pale blond hair away from her face. "If you keep the loads evenly distributed, you shouldn't have a problem."

"Problem?"

"Llamas express their displeasure by spitting, but that's really a llama-llama thing."

"Come on, Rory," he replied, only slightly reassured. "I'll put the bags in place. You tie them." He headed cautiously toward a piebald llama.

"Dad, meet Fred."

Fred emitted a sound like high tension wires that Garrett could only hope came from the front end of the beast.

"He's humming!" Rory looked thrilled to be among these strange-looking creatures. In that, he didn't take after his father. As a kid Garrett had never been allowed a pet.

"So, how do you keep them clean?" his son asked Samantha. "I can't picture giving one of these guys a bath."

"They'd get bathed only if I were going to show them," she replied. "Which I'm not. Everybody here stays happy with a lot of rolling in the dust on their part and some very careful brushing on mine. And spring shearing."

For the first time, the woman's speech pattern, her cultured inflection, fully registered with Garrett. He took note of her spotless designer jeans, her expensive boots and her carefully ironed shirt—some soft material in a grayish-green—nothing from the local discount store. Stuff Noelle would have picked out. The Weston woman seemed to know what she was doing with the llamas, but she sure didn't look or sound as if she belonged on a North Carolina farm.

"Can I do it as part of my job?" Rory asked her. "Brush 'em, I mean."

"I'll teach you if you really want. It's tricky. Llamas are very sensitive to touch. Their coats can be full of static. And more than that, you have to earn their trust…."

Garrett listened with surprise to his son and this stranger talking easily. Rory had spoken more words in the past five minutes than he had in the entire week he'd been in Applegate. As a father, he wanted to be a part of the conversation, too.

He fell back on what every resident asked a newcomer. "So, Samantha, where are you from originally?"

She looked as if he'd asked her for her Social Security and bank account numbers plus the key to her house. At that moment the instincts of both father and sheriff kicked in. It wouldn't be a bad idea to run a check on his son's employer.

Samantha tried to keep her features neutral. "I've lived too many places to count," she replied with her pat answer. It wasn't a lie. Although the Virginia estate outside D.C. had always been the family home, as an adult she'd traveled the world for the hotel business.

"Army brat?"

Rechecking a cinch, she pretended not to have heard the question.

"How do you come to run a llama trekking business in western North Carolina?" he persisted.

She wasn't about to tell him about the rehab center just outside Asheville, recommended by an old family friend, and its program, wherein residents took turns caring for a Noah's ark assortment of animals. She'd fallen in love with Pogo the llama. Actually, she'd fallen in love with the calm and purposeful woman she'd become in the llama's presence.

She inspected a strap Rory had tightened. "Good work," she said, then turned to the sheriff. "Who wouldn't want to do this if they had the opportunity?"

As he lifted the last piece of baggage from the ground, the glance he gave her said he knew she was being deliberately evasive. But he didn't pursue the issue.

She took the pack from his hands and headed for Percy as the sound of the Rockbrook Camp van floated up the road. *Good.* She didn't need any more questions from Sheriff McQuire. Nor any more looks. If her father was a steamroller in a tux, and her ex-almost-fiancé a fox in the henhouse, she suspected this man was a walking, talking lie detector. She preferred staying off his register.

"It seems like you have things under control," he said, his manner brusque. "Son, see you at supper."

"Okay." Rory eyed the giggling girls piling out of the van with as much trepidation as Samantha felt for his father's questions. "I'm gonna clean up that garbage in the pasture near the road." And before the lead camper could reach him, he bolted.

Samantha didn't see the sheriff leave. She made herself busy settling the girls and giving them the basic instructions that would lead to a happy trail experience. As she talked, as she demonstrated what to do, over the girls' questions and the llamas' gentle humming, she began to feel at ease. Despite the possibility that her parents or the paparazzi could invade her sanctuary at any moment or that Rory's father could reveal her as a fraud, she refused to be driven from her new life. These campers didn't care that she was an heiress. This land didn't care that she was a recovering alcoholic. Her llamas didn't care about her background as a deb. They cared about her present behavior. A kind word. A gentle touch. Those were things that Samantha could offer from the heart. It was an authentic start. She would not let others spoil it.

THOUGHTS OF NOELLE AND RORY and the perplexing new owner of Whistling Meadows weighing on his mind, Garrett eased his cruiser up the rutted trail on the Whittaker property—one of many old logging roads that crisscrossed the area. Lily Whittaker had called him to say her son Mack had taken his shotgun and a full bottle of Jack Daniel's and had left the house without a word. She was worried. It wasn't hunting season.

Garrett was worried, too.

Mack Whittaker had been his best deputy. And his best friend. Hired because of his army training, Mack had successfully juggled work for the Sheriff's Department with a continued Armed Forces commitment in the reserves. He had seen active duty in the reserves in a call-up to Iraq. Garrett had promised him his position when he got back. Trouble was, Stateside again, Mack didn't seem to want the job anymore. Or Garrett's friendship. Or any part of his previous life. He'd broken up with his longtime girlfriend. His mama said he was a bear to live with. His daddy said his eyes looked like those of a dead man.

After one nasty brawl in town, he shunned old friends and acquaintances entirely. People reported seeing him in odd places, on foot tramping the side of the roads, sometimes crossing fields, sometimes lying way up on Lookout Rock, motionless, a bottle in his hand. He rarely drove. He never spoke.

Garrett approached their boyhood hideout with caution. He knew what worried Lily most, but if Mack had taken a full bottle of whiskey, he wasn't planning on doing away with himself before he did away with the contents of that bottle. Drunk, however, Mack might turn the shotgun on an intruder.

Garrett didn't feel like an intruder here. The big old cave had been Mack's and his fortress as boys. Garrett's refuge. His foster parents had been conscientious enough, sometimes even kind, but Garrett had never felt he fit in anywhere until the first day of school in third grade when Mack had come to his defense on the playground. Even at eight, Mack had had an inordinate sense of fair play. After that the two had been like brothers.

The man staggering on the ledge in front of the cave, however, didn't look like Garrett's brother or his friend. Unshaven, hair wild, dirty clothes in disarray, Mack looked like a vagrant ready for a sober-up stay in jail.

"Get out of here!" he shouted as Garrett stepped

out of the cruiser. "Don't want your sermons. Or your pity."

"When did I ever preach to you?" Garrett stood not ten feet away. He could see the half-empty bottle of booze and the shotgun lying on the pebble-strewn ground. He wasn't leaving without either his friend or the gun. "But you've been back a month now. Don't you think it's time you let someone know what's gnawing at your gut?"

Mack sank against the mossy embankment near the cave entrance. "Even if I told you, you couldn't begin to understand."

"Try me." Garrett suspected part of Mack's despair was that he'd returned from war while one of his unit—one of their high school classmates, Nate Donahue—had not.

"Sheriff—" the word was spoken with uncustomary contempt "—you live in a mighty small world. In little ol' Applegate you think you have a handle on right and wrong, black and white, up and down. But I'm here to tell you you're one misinformed sombitch."

"Sounds like you're the one offering up the sermon."

Mack said nothing.

"Rory's home," Garrett said, trying to break through to his friend. From the minute of Rory's birth, Mack had embraced the role of uncle. "He's been asking after you."

"What'd you tell him?"

"I don't know what to tell him. Do you want to see him?"

"No."

"Okay. I get your point. You look like hell. Why don't you come back to the barracks with me? Have a shower and shave. It's McMillan's turn to cook. Chili. Everybody would be glad to see you." He kept talking even though it was obvious Mack was tuning him out. If Mack wanted to wall himself off after what he'd been through, who was Garrett to judge? But he was determined not to give up on his buddy. "Come on."

Mack shook his head.

"Suit yourself. I'll leave you the bottle, but your daddy needs the shotgun to take care of a wood-chuck that's been raiding your mama's garden."

Mack narrowed bleary eyes. "His case of hunting rifles isn't enough?"

"Apparently not." Garrett picked up the weapon.

Mack didn't resist. Instead, he closed his eyes and leaned his head back against the embankment. When he spoke, his words were low and menacing. "There are a thousand and one ways to destroy life, and none of 'em needs a shotgun."

The satisfaction Garrett had felt at retrieving the gun drained right out of him. "Sure you couldn't use some chili?"

"What I could use, friend, you can't supply."

"I'll be back, anyway."

"Don't bother."

"You know me better than that."

"I know nothing anymore."

This statement—from a guy who had always been confident in who he was and his place in the world—made Garrett's blood run cold. He wouldn't argue now, but he'd keep returning until Mack showed signs of the man he'd once been.

With a heavy heart Garrett got in the car. Thank God he still knew who he was. Sheriff. And father. And regarding the latter, he needed to take care of matters he could still control. He needed to get in touch with Noelle. Maybe she hadn't made a decision about Rory's schooling. Kids could hear a suggestion and blow it all out of proportion. When he did reach her, his ex would want to know what their son was doing with his summer so far. Noelle might be highly focused on her career, but she was also a fiercely devoted, often overprotective mother. He wanted to be able to reassure her Rory's job was safe and his employer reliable. She, too, would want a background check on Samantha Weston.

While driving back to headquarters, he phoned Noelle. Surprisingly, she picked up immediately. "Garrett, hello. I was expecting your call. Is Rory okay?"

"He's fine. For the most part." He tried to choose his words carefully. "He seems to think boarding school is a done deal, however, and he's not happy about that. I can't say I'm too pleased about it, either. You could have consulted me."

"I threw out the idea of Harpswell, among others, to get Rory thinking about the broader possibilities in his future."

"Broader than?" Garrett didn't trust the implications of the *broader* concept. Not long after they'd married, Noelle had begun to chafe under what she considered their constricting life in Applegate. "He's going to be an eighth-grader. How much broader than decent grades, friends and an interest in the world around him—animals, for instance—does his life have to get?"

He could hear her sigh from clear across the Atlantic.

"Less restricting than North Carolina," she said at last.

"Are you moving?"

"I didn't want to discuss it with you or Rory until I had something solid to add to the list of possibilities. But, yes, a move might be in the future. I'm here interviewing for a position—a promotion—in our London headquarters."

He had to pull his cruiser to the side of the road. Had to tamp down his rising anger. "And you want to put our kid in a boarding school so you can take a job overseas? What's wrong with the possibility of letting him live with me?"

"That would be one of the choices. As is boarding school. But I was really hoping you'd support me in trying to convince Rory it would be a wonderful experience to live in London. It would be an education in itself."

"You want to take him with you?"

"Of course. But I want him to want to come."

"Even farther away from me."

"You would have summers together. That wouldn't change."

But how much would Rory change in a year's time? Garrett didn't want to be a stranger to his son.

"Besides, there's e-mail and the telephone," Noelle insisted. "Letters even. And you could always fly to England." She made it sound so simple. Made him sound so provincial for not immediately embracing such simplicity.

"The three of us need to discuss this."

"Absolutely. But don't jump the gun. I haven't been offered the job. Yet."

With her talent and drive, he had no doubt she would be.

"I have to run." Her voice was charged with the thrill of a challenge. "Wish me luck."

"Luck," he replied without enthusiasm, wondering, sourly, if wanting to have a good, solid father-son relationship here in Applegate meant limiting Rory.

He and Noelle hadn't even talked about how happy he was to be working at Whistling Meadows.

THE ROCKBROOK VAN DEPARTED AS Red's pickup, the bed loaded with bulging garbage bags, arrived in the barnyard. Rory got out, but Red leaned through the driver's window. "I'm hauling this to the landfill," he said, then added with a nod to Rory, "The kid can work."

"So I see," Samantha replied, surprised Rory had pulled Red out of retirement.

"Someone dumped all this in the pasture by the road." The boy wrinkled up his face. "Who would do that?"

Red smiled. "I tried to tell him some kids around here think summer activities mean dumping garbage, smashing mailboxes and toilet papering the trees along Main Street. Seems they do things differently in Charlotte."

"You might have a dog problem, too," Rory said. "We walked the fence line and saw signs of digging."

Red's smile disappeared. "Most likely those would be Tanner's dogs."

Samantha didn't like the sound of that. If dogs got

in the pasture, they could wreak havoc with the llamas. "Isn't there a leash law?"

"You'd need to ask the sheriff," Red replied. "If there is, no one pays attention to it. I'll stop by Tanner's on my way to the dump and talk to him about keeping his hounds on his own property."

"No," Samantha said quickly. From experience in the hotel business, she'd come to realize the importance of being an upfront neighbor to those already in the area. "I'll talk to him."

"I don't know if that would be a good idea." Red seemed just as adamant. "Tanner isn't what you'd call open to suggestion."

"We'll do fine." At the Singapore Ashley, she'd dealt with everyone from architects to contractors to lawyers to local officials and merchants. Tanner Harris couldn't be more difficult than any of them. "I'll bicycle over right now."

"I'll go with you," Rory offered. "I don't know Red's nephew, but I know dogs."

Red eyed the two of them. "As long as you both remember the cur you have to watch out for is Tanner."

Samantha checked that the inner pasture gate was latched—the llamas, released from their packs and tethers, were already letting off steam, chest butting and rolling in the dust—then wheeled her bike out of the barn.

Rory joined her. "How was today's trek?"

"It was the beginner course. Just a few hours of hiking up to Lookout Rock and back with some trail mix and sports drinks thrown in for good measure. But the girls had fun."

"They were noisy."

"They were okay on the trail. I think the giggling beforehand was mostly for your benefit."

She hadn't meant to make him blush, but he did anyway, then sped up ahead of her.

Following him to her neighbor's property, she turned in at the corner of the fence where her pasture gave way to a woebegone yard. There, three hulking teenagers worked at building a trailer of sorts from lumber and spare parts. An all-terrain vehicle and two dirt bikes were parked nearby. Four large dogs lay chained to a tree. Rory stopped at the edge of the road and warily eyed the scene.

"Hello!" Samantha called out. "Is your father home?"

"No," came a mumbled response before the dogs clambered to their feet and began a raucous baying. The three young men worked on without looking up.

Not knowing how long the dogs' chains were, Samantha stayed put. Rory inched closer to her in what seemed more of a protective gesture than fear.

"Hush!" one of the boys shouted, making a menacing gesture with a wrench. As a group, the dogs slunk back to the tree.

"I'm Samantha Weston. Your new neighbor. May I have a word with you?"

The tallest teenager slowly straightened. "It's a free country."

Pulling one of her business cards from her back pocket, she left her bike at the edge of the road. "Would you, please, have your father call me? My number's on the card."

The boy took the card and, without looking at it, stuffed it in his jeans. "I don't think any of us are interested in goin' on a hike with llamas." The last word was said with great contempt.

"I'm not trying to drum up business. I wanted to talk about the importance of keeping dogs out of the pasture."

"You got a fence."

"We've found signs of digging."

"Lots of animals round here." He jerked his head toward the dogs. "Ours are tied up."

"I appreciate it," she said evenly. "I want to be a good neighbor, too. Please, have your father phone me."

As she turned, he mumbled, "If you wanna be a good neighbor, why'd you cut off our access?"

"Access?"

"You had to see the trails we made."

She'd seen them. Ugly gashes worn over time with no regard for the land or its vegetation. "As I understand it," she said, keeping her voice even, "the county has provided new and extensive ATV trails."

"We had our own at Uncle Red's," a second boy added, standing in truculent solidarity with the first. "Until you came along."

"Now that you have better ones, you don't need my property anymore. But if you're interested, you can come over and meet the llamas. See what trail life without motors can be like."

The three gave a united snort of derision, then turned their backs and resumed work on the trailer.

Samantha returned to Rory and the bikes. "I'll ride with you into town. I want to talk to the feed store owner. See if he'd be willing to top-dress the cattle feed I buy with some other ingredients good for llama health."

"You're not worried?"

"About their health? No, they're doing fine on pasture for the summer."

"Not the llamas." Rory waited until they'd turned a bend in the road. "Those guys back there."

"I think they're harmless. Ticked off, yes. But harmless. I hear the new ATV trails are really good. They'll get used to not having a backyard playground."

Rory looked unconvinced. "You're lucky you have me and Red."

Samantha was touched by his gallantry.

"Then there's always my dad if we run into real trouble."

Oh, no, she didn't need the sheriff in her new, clean-as-a-whistle life. "There won't be trouble," she reassured him.

The Harrises were the least of her concerns. Yes, she needed to discuss a new grain mixture with the feed store owner, but, more important, she needed to ask about the curt message he'd left on her voice mail—that a man had been asking about her in town. A member of the paparazzi or her father's detective, Max?

Neither possibility was good news.

CHAPTER THREE

TUCKED IN A VALLEY OFF THE beaten track, partway between Brevard and Asheville, Applegate was little like its bigger neighbors, the first a college town, the second a tourist destination. And although gentrification was slowly making inroads, one couldn't spot the changes from the rustic interior of Abel Nash's feed store. Samantha stood amid the stacked burlap sacks of grain and scarred wooden bins of seeds, waiting to speak to the owner and trying desperately not to sneeze on the fine dust that hung in the air. She couldn't help but wonder why the sheriff stood sentry outside the store, looking for all the world as if he was waiting for someone in particular.

"Samantha, what can I do for you?" At last Abel turned his attention to her.

From her pocket she pulled a slip of paper on which she'd written the specifics of the new feed she wanted. "Could you give me this blend with my next delivery?"

He glanced at the list. "No problem. Anything else?"

"About your message…"

"That guy nosing around, yeah." Abel scowled.

"Did he give a name?"

"No. He was slippery that way. Gut feeling, I didn't trust him."

"How so?"

"Said he was trying to find his long-lost niece. Showed me a picture of some society woman. Ashley something-or-other. Come to think of it, she had a passing resemblance to you—kind of like a gussied up cousin—but his niece? I sure as heck wouldn't put the two of them on the same family shrub, let alone tree. He looked like a forties gangster."

Samantha suppressed a smile. Not a newshound, at least. But Max. While it was true her father's detective looked rough around the edges, the man had a heart of gold. Nevertheless, she didn't want "Uncle Max" meddling in her new life. Not at this tender stage.

"What did you tell him?" she asked, fearing Abel Nash owed her, a newcomer, scant loyalty.

"I asked him if I looked like I ran in her circle. Then I told him if he didn't need any seed or feed, I had paying customers to wait on." He paused as if weighing his words. "You'll find this has always been a live-and-let-live town. We're not overfond of snoops."

That was putting it mildly. In doing research on the area, as far back as the revolutionary war,

Samantha had found that this region, with its peaks and valleys and inaccessible hollows, had been a haven for staunch individualists and rebels and people with something to hide. "I appreciate your respect for privacy," she replied.

Abel had given nothing away, but surely Max had talked to others in town. Had they been as circumspect? She glanced at the sheriff on the sidewalk. Fortunately, Max, in keeping a low profile, always worked without benefit of law enforcement. He had other means. Unfortunately, he often proved more tenacious and more thorough than his uniformed counterparts. She'd almost rather take her chances with Garrett McQuire.

Almost.

Abel cleared his throat. "You're a woman alone. If you don't already have a gun, you might think of getting one."

The idea appalled her, and her face must have registered that reaction.

"Most people do around here," he said. "If for no other reason than to protect their livestock. Against snakes and coyotes. Intruders."

"I never thought…"

"Consider it," the storekeeper urged, not unkindly.

The responsibility of individual gun ownership. The necessity. A daunting concept. In the hotel business, security was handled by…well, security. A staff discreet and out of sight. And always at the ready. Until this moment she hadn't really considered how others had taken care of her every need. And she'd considered herself an independent woman. Unsettled, she turned to go, only to discover she'd have to make her way past the sheriff still standing outside the door. An even more formidable prospect than purchasing a gun.

Why did he make her nervous even when she had nothing to hide? Nothing of substance. Not really.

She squared her shoulders and prepared to breeze by him with a cursory greeting. But stepping from the dim interior of the feed store into the bright June sunlight, she was temporarily blinded, and stopped to get her bearings.

"Can I have a word with you?" His deep voice, held firmly in check, nonetheless threatened her equilibrium. "I'd like to talk about Rory."

"He…he finished work for today. We rode our bikes into town together. Said he was going off with friends to swim."

"I know. He dropped by the office. Have you eaten lunch?"

She didn't want lunch with this man, but her stomach—last fed hours ago at a crack-of-dawn breakfast—took that moment to cast its own vote with a loud growl.

"I'll take that as a no." Before she could protest, he cupped her elbow and guided her across the street. She was stunned to discover he was leading her not to Rachel's Diner, but next door to the sheriff's office.

"I hope you like chili," he said as he propelled her through the front door. "McMillan made enough for an army."

That reminded Samantha of the children's taunt, "Who's gonna make me? You and whose army?" and wondered how much she'd have to reveal of herself during this "lunch."

Garrett was determined to get some answers from Samantha Weston—if that's who she really was—and he was going to do it on his own turf. He needed to balance her right to privacy with his need to know whom his son interacted with. The lunch invitation was meant to make the procedure—one that required finesse, something he wasn't sure he possessed—less threatening. He might be sheriff, but he'd been raised Southern. You didn't scare off a newcomer just because you didn't know what her daddy, granddaddy and great-granddaddy did for a living. Didn't know *yet*.

"Up this way." He motioned to a staircase that led to the barracks above the ground-floor offices.

Cool caution seemed to form a shield around her

as she climbed the stairs ahead of him. Clearly, she was on guard, and he wondered why. She paused, uncertain, at the top of the stairs.

Without introductions, he propelled her toward the kitchenette, past several deputies eating at the long central trestle table. They eyed Samantha with interest. It was unusual for him to bring an outsider up here. Business dealings he always conducted below and by the book. Any personal life he kept separate from his work. Maybe this wasn't such a good idea, after all.

Silently, he put together two trays of dishes, silverware, napkins, then indicated the chili, salad, bread, sweet tea. Holding herself regally, she responded with a nod that, yes, she'd try some of each. He hadn't felt so uncomfortable since his first middle school dance. The silence of the deputies behind them was deafening.

Handing her a tray, he headed for the stairs once more. She seemed mildly surprised they wouldn't be eating at the communal table—as if he'd ever let that happen.

"We can eat and talk in my office," he said in a low voice, but not low enough. He saw the corner of Deputy Sooner's mouth quirk in the beginning of a grin.

Safely downstairs in his office, he lowered his tray to the top of a stack of papers covering his blotter, then cleared a place opposite for hers. Pulling Rory's backpack from the only other chair in the room, he indicated she should sit. She did, gingerly, looking down at an empty trap Ziggy Newsome had returned after relocating a raccoon that had taken up residence in the Newsome attic.

With his foot Garrett pushed the trap into the corner. "Sorry about the housekeeping."

"You said you wanted to talk about your son." She was unflappable, this one.

"I don't know how much he's told you about his situation," he said, trying for equally cool.

"He said he spends summers and vacations with you and the rest of the year with his mother in Charlotte. Beyond that we only talk about animals and running my business. In those areas he seems very mature for his age."

"Do you know much about kids?"

"No."

"All the more reason we should talk."

Slowly spreading a napkin on her lap, she raised one eyebrow and gave him an if-you-say-so look, but didn't answer otherwise. He was a crossword fanatic. In the paper that morning one of the answers had been *hauteur.* At this moment the clue could have been "Samantha Weston."

"I guess because Rory splits his time between

my ex and me," he said, "we're twice as vigilant. As parents."

"That—" she took a delicate nibble of her salad "—and the fact you're sheriff and would naturally want to know who's moving into your territory and what they're planning on doing. Say, me."

"You've read me accurately there. And just about ninety-nine percent of the rest of the town. You had to know your business would stir up curiosity. It's unusual."

"And here Abel just got through telling me this is a live-and-let-live town." She shot him a command-the-room smile. "Are llama treks a suspicious activity, sheriff? I filed a prospectus when I applied for my permit. It's public information."

"I read it."

"Oh?" She paused, her fork halfway to her mouth. "Did you read Rachel's when she bought the diner? Or Abel's when he inherited the feed store?"

He found himself unaccountably taken back by her direct gaze and her cross-examination. "You… need to understand I'm talking to you as a father. I'd check out any situation I let my son into. Be it a sleepover with friends or a part-time job at Mickey D's—"

"So you want to know what kind of employer I am? Have you talked to Red Harris? I think he's observed me long and hard enough to provide a pretty good character reference. Or maybe Abel. He could tell you I pay my bills on time." Her tone was pseudo-light with a defensiveness that swam just below the surface. Her body language said he wasn't intimidating her. "Have you interviewed them?"

"No." Who the hell was conducting this interview? He bristled at her ability to turn the tables. "But now you bring up the matter of background checks, why's there no record for Samantha Weston? Not even a driver's license."

"So you did snoop on me." She seemed almost relieved. "FYI, there's no license under my name because I don't drive. Your lunch is getting cold."

He looked at the untouched meal in front of him. So much for finesse and the excuse of getting to know his son's employer.

"I think Rory and I are going to get along fine." She seemed to have no trouble eating and talking. With an unhurried elegance that would fit right in at a formal luncheon at the Grove Park Inn, she'd finished half her meal. "If you'd like, you could come with him to work one day. To observe."

"You really don't know much about twelve-year-olds, do you? He'd be mortified."

"Ah, yes. So much easier to investigate me."

"Come on now. Let's not get off on the wrong foot."

"But you did run a background check on me. Beyond the license."

He got the feeling this woman could hold her own. Anywhere. "Yes."

"And would you tell me what you found out?" she asked politely, as if they were discussing the weather for an upcoming polo match.

Screw finesse. "That everything from your phone bills to ownership of Whistling Meadows traces back to a corporation. Ashley Dreams, Inc."

"Yes," she replied without offering further explanation. "Is there anything wrong with that?"

"Not that I could see."

"Well, I guess I can't blame a man for doing his job." Her tone said otherwise.

"Just out of curiosity, what's your connection to Ashley Dreams?"

"Is this a sheriff question or a father question?" He noticed her brown eyes were flecked with gold. And they got darker the more serious she became.

"Neither. Just a question."

"You want to know if I'm the CEO or the hired help. Is that what you're getting at?"

One thing was certain, this woman was no one's hired help.

"Let's put it this way," she continued. "On paper Whistling Meadows is owned by Ashley Dreams,

Incorporated, but no one really owns that slice of pasture land and mountain. You should know that, sheriff. Your son says you grew up here. Its geologic history alone reaches so far back no human can really claim it. The llamas sense that if the people can't. The animals just live on the surface. Day to day. Content to be here amid the splendor. I suspect they chuckle at the idea that someone—corporation or individual—thinks he or she owns them or the land. But they humor us. Me, I'm just part of the scenery. Trying to live on Whistling Meadows without leaving too intrusive a footprint."

"A philosopher," he said, noting rather cynically she hadn't come close to answering his question.

"Now that's the nicest thing I've been called in a long time." She rose. "On that positive note, I need to get back to the farm. Thanks for lunch."

She smiled, then left his office, leaving him with a cold meal, the hint of some sophisticated fragrance she'd been wearing and the firm conviction that, philosopher or not, Samantha Weston—if that's who she really was—was one self-contained woman.

Outside, Samantha shook herself as if chilled. She was so mad she could bite someone. And wouldn't her mother be shocked at even the thought of such behavior. Well, this wasn't the Orchid Court at the Singapore Ashley. It wasn't even the breakfast room back home in Virginia. This was Main Street, Applegate, North Carolina, and the sheriff seemed to think he could be rude—rude and nosy—and get away with it.

So much for Abel's assessment that the town didn't abide snoops. Outside snoops, perhaps. The homegrown ones seemed to come with a badge.

Trying to let off steam, she pedaled her bike furiously back to the farm.

So what was she to do about the sheriff? What she always did with rude people. Ignore them. But what about Rory? With him working for her, she upped her chances of running into his father. She could fire the boy. And his "vigilant" guardian would probably seek legal redress. Wouldn't he think he'd discovered the pot of gold at the end of a rainbow when he realized how much she was worth?

No, she'd have to fly under the radar. With both the sheriff and Max on her trail…damn, she'd forgotten about Max. One thing was certain, he wouldn't have forgotten about her. That she hadn't seen him in town meant only one thing—he'd found out what he wanted and was headed back to her father to report. Then her daddy would take his time. He hadn't built his hotel empire by being rash. The grand opening of the Singapore Ashley would occupy him for a week or two. Maybe. If she was lucky. He wouldn't mention anything to her mother, not until the very moment he'd say, "Throw a few things in a bag for a little getaway." Then the two would sweep south. And Samantha's new life would be turned topsy-turvy by the whirlwind that always accompanied her parents. She could just picture Mother in the farmhouse. She'd do an extreme makeover in no time. And Father? She couldn't quite imagine him and Red and martinis on the bunkhouse porch.

Despite her request for time, her parents *would* arrive. Like a tsunami. There was absolutely nothing Samantha could do to stop them. She only hoped the press wouldn't follow.

Wouldn't that give the sheriff something to investigate?

As she turned her bicycle into the lane running up to Whistling Meadows, she realized she'd worked up quite a sweat under the June sun. How unladylike. Well, Mother would have to get used to her daughter's adaptation to the rigors of country living. And Samantha would simply have to not think about tomorrow. *Stay in the moment,* she chided herself. *Right now, neither the press nor your parents are here. Right now, there is no reason for you to see the sheriff. Right now…*there appeared to be a body on her front porch.

Yes, a man. Sprawled. Unmoving.

She looked toward the bunkhouse. Red's truck

was gone. Instinctively, she moved to page hotel security, then gave herself a reality check. Her next move was to call 9-1-1 and pray the sheriff didn't think she'd added murder to her sketchy résumé.

CHAPTER FOUR

"Is he dead?"

"Dead drunk." Garrett surveyed Mack, collapsed and motionless, on Samantha's porch. How had he managed to walk here from the Whittaker property with all that whiskey in him?

"Do you know who he is?" Samantha looked at Garrett with an extraordinary degree of equanimity. He could think of several women in town whom he'd known since childhood, yet those very women would be all bent out of shape in this situation. Had been in similar situations.

"I know him," he replied, unwilling to give out too much information. "Mack Whittaker." He began to calculate what it would take to get his friend's six-four, two-hundred-pound-plus frame into the cruiser. Although the men were equally matched size-wise, Garrett was at a disadvantage when Mack was unconscious and Garrett was doing all the work.

"Is someone missing him?" Without so much as

wrinkling her nose, Samantha knelt beside Mack's none-too-clean form. Garrett found himself staring at the curls of blond hair floating around her face, found himself noting that her porcelain complexion wasn't the norm around here. He worried a little at the hint of sunburn across her nose and cheeks, before catching himself. She looked up at him. Her eyes were actually the softest shade of hazel, not brown as he'd first thought, but her gaze was penetrating. "A wife maybe?"

"N-no. No wife. Parents." He pulled himself back into professional mode. "But I don't want Miss Lily to see her son like this. She's worried enough about him as is. I'll call for backup. Let him sleep it off in a jail cell. Clean him up when he wakes."

"Is he dangerous?"

"No." He didn't want to add, *only to himself.* It would be an admission on Garrett's part of how low his old buddy had sunk, of how grim the road to recovery seemed and how little Garrett had been able to help. He wasn't ready to throw in the towel yet, even if Mack was.

"Then let him stay here," she said, standing. As if she was in charge. In fact, the way she spoke, the way she carried herself, said she was accustomed to giving orders. And used to having those orders followed.

"You don't even know him."

"But I know something about—"

Red Harris drove up then, interrupting their conversation. Too bad. Garrett couldn't imagine how Samantha could possibly relate to this sorry-looking piece of humanity taking up floor space on her porch. As different from her as night and day.

Red jumped out of his truck. "Ziggy Newsome told me he saw Mack heading this way. None too steady on his feet, he said." With concern on his craggy features, he studied Samantha. "Did he scare you, Duchess?"

"I'm okay now. But at first I thought he was dead."

"He couldn't look much worse if he was." Red turned to Garrett. "You want help gettin' him in the car?"

"Yeah. Thanks."

"Wait!" Samantha put out a hand to stop them. "I still think he should stay here. Until he sobers up."

"Don't take this the wrong way," Garrett replied, squatting to get a grip under Mack's armpits, "but you're crazy. A jail cell's the place for him until he comes round."

"On second thought, maybe she isn't crazy," Red countered, hefting Mack from under his knees. "He'd be right pissed with you if he woke up in front of coworkers. Humiliated. Let's carry him to the bunkhouse. I'll keep an eye on him."

Garrett was still skeptical. "You don't have to do this, Red."

"I know I don't. But everyone—me included—has a story about Mack helping 'em at one time or another. He's good people. Laid a little low, is all."

Samantha seemed to hang on every word.

Garrett could fully understand Red's feelings, but he couldn't get a handle on hers.

"Duchess," Red said, "get the bunkhouse door for us. The sheriff and I'll haul Mack along as best we can."

Even with the two of them, they had to sidle cautiously, Mack's dead weight hanging between them. Inside the old bunkhouse Samantha stood beside a bed in the corner of what used to be the foreman's room.

"Not there!" Red exclaimed. "That's my bed and I just put on fresh sheets. I may be a Good Samaritan, but I'm no saint. Let's get him on a bunk in the workers' dorm, next room over."

Garrett was glad to finally lay Mack down. That whole "He ain't heavy, he's my brother" saying was a crock.

"You'll let me know when he's conscious?" Samantha asked Red. "I want to talk to him."

"Sure."

She then turned to Garrett. "I'll see you to your cruiser."

"No need." He wondered what Samantha could possibly have to say to Mack.

Despite the brush-off, she followed anyway. "This man works for the sheriff's department?"

"He's on leave." It wasn't any of her business. Besides, he didn't like being questioned. Especially about things beyond his control. "Plus, he's a buddy from way back. So…what's *your* interest?"

She leveled her cool gaze at him. There was strength and resolve beneath that sophisticated exterior. You could tell by being three minutes in her company. What he didn't know—yet—was what made her tick. Why she'd picked Applegate in the first place. Why, after being a quiet newcomer to this point, she'd chosen to get involved with Mack, of all people.

"Do you want us to call you?" she asked, "When—Mack, did you say?—is in better shape?"

"I'll circle back in a while. If you wait until he gets his feet under him, he may be gone before you know it."

"Perhaps." She looked as if she knew something about his old friend that he didn't.

"I'll check in later anyway."

"No need," she insisted in an echo of his own words earlier. "Red and I are good."

Dissatisfied, he got in the car. This morning he'd set two goals at the top of his mental to-do list: help

Mack and run a background check on Rory's employer. And what had he accomplished at the end of the day? Damn little.

Samantha watched the sheriff leave. Having deliberately sought solitude to put her life back together, why had she stuck out her neck just then?

Trying to avoid her own question, she made her way to the barn to ready the equipment for tomorrow's lunch-and-wine trek with a group of retirees from Atlanta. She wanted everything to be a go when she got back from her early-morning AA meeting.

Not five minutes into her work, Percy poked his head over the pasture-side half door. Ever since she'd brought him into the paddock two weeks ago to treat a split and infected toenail, he'd decided he liked her company more than his fellow pack animals' and had shown an uncanny propensity to act more human than llama. And more nosy than most. Today it was apparent he was going to stick around to see what was what.

What, exactly, *was* what?

Why had she come out of hiding to help Mack Whittaker? The sheriff's buddy, no less. As Percy eyed her, she told herself she wasn't hiding. She told herself Samantha Weston wasn't an alias. Samantha had been her paternal grandmother's first name, and Weston her maternal grandmother's maiden name. She hoped combining and using the two now was less lie and more homage to a pair of women who had led purposeful lives. She wanted to do the same.

And if you led a purposeful life, you didn't just let a fellow human being self-destruct as Mack seemed intent on doing. She recognized his pain. Maybe it was time she dug deep inside herself, to see how strong she really was, to see what she had to offer.

A daunting proposition.

"Mind your own business," she said to Percy, who continued to stare at her. Llamas could seem unsettlingly perceptive. "Go hang out with the boys."

He didn't, and she finished her business in the barn under his soulful gaze.

True to his word, Garrett returned later that evening, but he checked in at the bunkhouse without as much as a hello to her. She told herself it was just as well. Of course, she was telling herself a lot of things lately, some of them helpful, but many of them obvious rationalizations.

EARLY WEDNESDAY MORNING Garrett drove Rory to work at Whistling Meadows only to be met by Red.

"We need to see to the fence—" the older man said to Rory, hefting the bicycle out of the trunk "—before the Duchess gets back. Someone damaged a length of it by ramming it with a tractor or an ATV, maybe. I have my suspicions as to who mighta done it, but I'll take care of those in my own good time. I've got the fence supplies in my truck. Let's get a move on."

"I'll go see Mack," Garrett said.

"He's not here," Red replied, wheeling Rory's bike to the side of the porch. "The Duchess took him to her AA meeting."

"Her AA meeting?"

"She goes like clockwork every morning after early chores."

That little bomb had barely gone off when Garrett thought of something else. "But she doesn't drive, and Mack—"

"Her sponsor picks her up." Red got in his truck and Rory followed. "Don't worry about Mack. He's in good hands. The Duchess may look like a china doll, but she's one tough cookie."

Standing in a cloud of dust as Red drove away, Garrett didn't know what perplexed him more. That elegant and in-control Samantha attended AA, or that she'd succeeded in getting Mack to accept help. Where he'd failed. Suddenly, he felt his world slip sideways. Not only had his best friend put himself in the hands of a stranger, but his son was working his first real job—had taken off just now without a backward glance—even as his ex-wife plotted a new life overseas. None of this involved Garrett, and it stung.

It wasn't that he needed to feel in charge. He just wanted some say in the matter. And on those three issues he had none.

As the week progressed, he felt even less in control. More in the dark.

In the parking lot of the Piggly Wiggly, he ran into Mack's mama and helped her load her groceries into her car. She said her son had called to tell her not to worry. He was sobering up at Whistling Meadows. Attending AA. Miss Lily had tears in her eyes as she professed it a miracle. Garrett had felt a twinge. It seemed being a parent didn't get any easier with time. He also didn't see any reason to stick his nose into Mack's business if Samantha and Red really were helping. Anyway, Mack hadn't called him.

Rory increasingly went to work earlier and stayed later. One day Garrett came across his son and Red putting up new signs advertising the llama treks. They said someone had pulled down all the old signs. Both seemed to take the petty act of vandalism personally. At home, Rory spent his time in his room, pouring over a pile of animal husbandry books and pamphlets he'd borrowed from county extension.

Garrett had talked to Noelle once more. She'd said the interview had gone well, but the bank was committed to a deep search before making the final decision. She wasn't worried and had stuck around London long enough for some advantageous schmoozing, then had flown home to Charlotte to get back in the Stateside rat race. When the subject of Rory's job came up, Noelle had said she was counting on Garrett to fully vet this Weston woman.

Trouble was, Garrett had mixed feelings about a further search into Samantha's background. She had Red's full support, and Red was no fool. So she attended AA. That was her business. She didn't even own a car, leaving Rory in no danger there. All her permits were in order. As sheriff and father, how much more did he need to know? Nothing, if truth be told. But as a man—

"You sure that item's part of your purchase, Sheriff?" Piggly Wiggly cashier Kate Mulroney's voice cut into his thoughts.

He looked down to see a box of tampons along with his milk, bread and coffee on the checkout belt.

"Those would be mine." A slender hand pulled the tampons away.

He turned to find himself gazing into Samantha's eyes. Drawn, against his better judgment, to the cool mystery of the woman.

But Kate brought him back to his senses. "So tonight the town council's voting on my cousin's crazy proposal," she said as she rang up his purchases. "If it passes, you're going to have your hands full." Chuckling, she shook her head. "A road bowling tournament. Who ever heard of such a thing?"

"Actually, I have," Samantha said. "I think it originated in Ireland."

"So my cousin Pat says," Kate replied, eager to carry on a three-way conversation while all Garrett wanted was for her to give him his receipt so that he could escape, get home, have supper with his kid, then wrestle him awhile for the remote before making an appearance at the council meeting. "He went to a Mulroney family reunion in West Virginia," Kate continued, unfazed by Garrett's impatience, "where they hosted a tournament. You'd have thought he'd made a pilgrimage to the old country. Came back Irish as all get out. Now wants to be called Padraig—"

"Kate," Garrett interjected, bagging his few items. "My receipt."

"No problem." She began to hand over the slip of paper. "Oh, wait. My bad. I rang up the tampons on your purchase. Go figure. I'll have to cancel out and begin again."

He grabbed the receipt. "I'll buy Ms. Weston her…stuff."

"Don't be ridiculous. We'll settle up outside," Samantha insisted, pushing him gently toward the exit.

That was no solution. He wanted to get away from her.

Outside, next to her bicycle, she appropriated the receipt, then dug into her jeans for the money. The soft breeze made her blond curls bounce, the sunlight made them shine. "What's this about a road bowling tournament?" she asked.

"How's Mack doing?" he countered.

"Fine." She looked him right in the eye as she handed back the receipt and exact change. "And the road bowling tournament?"

He really didn't want to discuss it. It was the kind of quirky event small towns were infamous for. The kind of occasion that used to make Noelle cringe and say she was surrounded by hillbillies. He would rather discuss Mack, but it was obvious Samantha didn't want to go there.

He pocketed her money. "Right now it's just Pat's pipe dream. Ask me again tomorrow if the town council gives it the okay." He strode off without a backward glance.

Samantha watched his stiff, retreating form. She knew she'd provoked his rudeness by not giving him a proper update on his friend Mack, but those were Mack's wishes. Having involved herself this far with his rehabilitation, she couldn't risk losing his trust.

She pedaled her bicycle home, thinking about

the two men. If she didn't know better, she'd think them fraternal twins. Dealing with both was like handling dynamite.

When she finally pulled to a stop in front of her house, she could see Mack and Red and Rory huddled together on the bunkhouse porch farther up the hill. They looked far too serious to be having a friendly game of cribbage. And why was Rory still here? It was nearly supper time. She was paying him for only four hours a day. Granted, they'd agreed his schedule could be flexible, but the boy seemed to live on the property. Not that she had any complaints. Right from the very beginning, he seemed to adopt an uncanny attitude of stewardship toward the llamas and the land. And Red—she didn't pay him anything—now seemed more intent on helping her make a go of Whistling Meadows than in retiring to his fishing. For a person whose original intention was to lie low, she was acquiring quite the ragtag commune.

Not yet hungry—the thought of her own cooking held little appeal—she hiked up toward the bunkhouse, along the fence marking the inner pasture where the llamas were rolling in the dust. Along the track Red's free-range chickens scattered, squawking, before her.

"Hello!" she called out as she approached the guys

on the porch. They quickly pulled apart. As if they'd been talking about her. "What's up?"

"Nothing," Red replied a little too quickly. "Anything new in town?"

"What's this about a road bowling tournament?" She really wanted to know. Anything that might bring people into town would be good for business, hers included. Not that profit was what this new venture was about, but old ways of thinking died hard.

Mack got up and, without so much as a nod in greeting, went into the bunkhouse.

"The road bowling tournament would be Pat Mulroney's idea," Red said. "And I'm thinking, if the plan passes the council, I might get up a team." He looked at Rory. "You in, sport?"

Rory looked interested. "A team?"

"If you could even call it that." Red leaned back in his chair as if to spin a yarn, and Samantha took a seat on the top porch step. "You need two people. They alternate throwing a two-pound iron ball down the road on a 'course' agreed upon beforehand. The team that comes in with the fewest throws wins."

"That's it?" Rory asked.

"That's pretty much it, as I understand the game," Samantha said. "There are almost no rules and no out-of-bounds whatsoever."

"But lots of pocket flasks," Red added. "That and the fact Pat says they didn't close the roads to traffic during the West Virginia tournament might make your pa a little nervous, Rory."

"Where do you get the iron balls?"

Red chuckled. "There's rumors the old cannon-balls in front of the courthouse are exactly two pounds. More for the sheriff to worry about if the tournament gets the green light."

Rory seemed undisturbed by the law-and-order logistics. "I think Whistling Meadows should have a team." He flexed a puny bicep. "Work's got me ripped. We can call ourselves the Whistling Meadows Wonders."

"Don't look at me!" Samantha said. "I can't even throw a Frisbee. But I'll spring for drinks. *Lemonade.*"

"Maybe we can convince Mack to partner with you," Red suggested. "You can call yourselves the Teetotalin' Twosome."

Samantha doubted that pairing. Mack was an enigma. Once she'd convinced him to attend AA with her, he'd approached rehabilitation with a vengeance. That didn't mean he communicated with her—other than to tell her not to talk about his business to anyone, specifically Garrett. In fact, there was something lifeless about Mack. Samantha worried that, AA or not, he hadn't faced the root of his despair. She wasn't sure she could see him rejoining the sheriff's department. She certainly couldn't imagine him participating in any road bowling high jinks. She had yet to see him even smile.

"I gotta shove off," Rory said. "Dad's home for supper tonight. Geneva's making pot roast. His favorite."

Oh, pot roast—that somebody else had made—sounded so good.

Samantha watched Rory race away on his bike as if he were trying out for NASCAR. "It's funny," she said. "I haven't had experience with kids, but I miss his energy when he's not on the farm."

Red eyed her intently. "Kids are a blessing."

"Do you have any?"

"No." His look became faraway. "It wasn't meant to be, I guess." He shook himself. "But you—"

"Don't even have a guy in the picture. I've watched your hens and rooster enough to know there has to be a likely man around."

"Seems there is a likely man."

"Are you flirting with me, Mr. Harris?"

"In my dreams." He shot her a lopsided grin. "You mean you haven't noticed the logical fella? The one right in front of you?"

"You can't possibly be talking about Mack."

"Not Mack."

Good. Because although Mack and she had spent some intense time together the past week, there was absolutely no chemistry. Not a fraction of the sexual tension she felt when she was in the company of—

"No! You can't mean the sheriff!"

"Yessirree!" Red's sun-wrinkled face was filled with enormous self-satisfaction. "I think the whole town's noticed the sparks when you and he just pass on the street."

"But I'm not looking for anyone!"

"Neither's he. I'm here to tell you the laws of nature don't care what plans either of you've made." He rose from his seat. "Guess I'd better see what can Mack wants me to open tonight. I'm thinkin' corned beef hash. See you later, Duchess."

Samantha sat on the porch step. Stunned. She and the sheriff were not mutually attracted.

Liar.

GARRETT LET HIMSELF INTO THE house after the town council meeting.

"How did things go?" Geneva asked, shrugging into her sweater, gathering her things to leave.

"They all thought the tournament was a great promotional idea. As if Applegate were some kind of sideshow."

"Oh, it'll be fun." Geneva shook her head. "I hear

Ziggy Newsome was going to suggest using the dirt road that runs up his hollow. Even away from the main traffic, you'll have your hands full."

Didn't he know it. "How's Rory?"

"Went to bed early. All that manual labor and fresh air's plum tuckered the boy out."

He checked his watch. Nine-fifteen? "It's good for him."

"He seems happy."

Garrett wouldn't know. Rory was seldom around enough anymore for a father to gauge his moods. "Thanks, Geneva. See you in the morning."

"Good night."

Restless—and not just because of the upcoming road bowling debacle—Garrett paced the small living room. He couldn't believe he'd spent the evening standing in the back of the council meeting room, thinking not about the logistics of traffic control and crowd control and liquor control, but of self-control. Where Samantha Weston was concerned. Lord, the woman was attractive.

And, he suspected, in a whole other league than the one in which he chose to play ball.

So what was he going to do about her constantly invading his thoughts—both waking and dreaming? If he had the guts, he'd ask her out. One date would prove how ill-suited for each other they were. And that should end the attraction. Crazy idea, sure, but it might just work.

He climbed the stairs to look in on Rory. Pushing open the bedroom door, he noted how his son no longer slept with a night-light. Noted, too, how both the window and screen were pushed up. Mosquitoes would eat the kid alive by dawn. Moving across the room to pull down the screen, he lingered at the foot of his son's bed, wanting to gaze on him in sleep as Rory would never allow awake. Under the covers, he seemed more bulked up than when he'd arrived for the summer. Maybe work on Samantha's farm was—

Wait a minute.

Garrett threw back the covers to discover not his son, but pillows craftily bunched to resemble a human form.

Where the hell was Rory?

CHAPTER FIVE

GARRETT STOOD IN RORY'S darkened room and told himself to think like a sheriff, not a father. If some parents called to tell him to put out an APB because their kid had sneaked out of the house after bedtime on a summer's night, he'd tell them first to calm down, then to call the kid's buddies.

But this was his own son.

And Rory, only in Applegate for vacations, had made few lasting friends except for Geneva's grand-sons—one a year older than Rory, one a year younger—who occasionally came in from Brevard to spend time with her. When they did, she brought them to work to keep Rory company. Garrett hadn't seen the boys in a couple weeks. Just the same, he whipped out his phone and punched in his housekeeper's cell number.

"Is everything all right?" she asked the second she picked up.

"No. Rory's gone." He flipped on the bedroom

light and scanned the room for a note or anything that indicated this was—God forbid—more than just a lark. "Did he give any indication this evening he was upset? Or maybe excited about meeting up with someone?" A girl? His son was the right age for this to be about a girl.

"He just seemed happy. Talked a blue streak about the farm. Those animals. That Weston woman. Said he needed a good night's sleep to get an early jump on work tomorrow."

Then, what the hell?

"I'm at the Piggly Wiggly right now," Geneva said. "Before I head home, I'll swing by the bowling lanes. See if he might be there. If not, I'll check the church parking lot. You know kids are always skateboarding there during the week."

"Thanks, Geneva, but you go straight home. Put your feet up. I'll call headquarters and ask those on patrol to be on the lookout."

"I won't relax till you call to tell me that boy is home safe and sound."

"I know." He shouldn't have bothered her.

Ringing off, he phoned the department. The dispatcher said she'd get the word out. Told him not to be concerned, that the sap was always rising in middle schoolers. Which only made him worry more.

A further hunt around Rory's room showed

Garrett that his son's backpack was gone. But his favorite baseball cap, his iPod and his electronic game collection were still there. Rory never traveled without those. It looked as if he planned to come back. But when? And where was he now?

Garrett suddenly remembered that this summer Noelle had sent their son to Applegate with a skinny, top-of-the-line cell phone with all the bells and whistles. At the time Garrett had thought it conspicuous excess for a twelve-year-old. Now, not seeing the phone anywhere in the room, he scanned his own listings for Rory's number. When it appeared, he hit Call, then paced the room as the dial tone rang once, twice, three times before switching to voice mail. He didn't bother to leave a message.

The cruiser was the next step. Downstairs he checked the back porch to confirm his suspicion that the bike was gone.

There was nothing to do but ride around, looking for his son. Even on a soft summer night, very few establishments were still open on Main Street at ten. Among them, the sheriff's department. The Piggly Wiggly. The Dairy Queen. The bowling lanes. As Garrett drove slowly and scanned the small clusters of kids, Rory was nowhere to be seen.

And then Garrett remembered something Geneva had said. About how, this evening, Rory had talked a blue streak about Whistling Meadows. Could he have gone there? Why? Concern for an animal? Garrett remembered how one summer Rory'd begged Garrett and Mack to let him sleep in a stall on the Whittaker farm to await the birth of a calf. But there had been no secrecy, no stealth that time.

He turned the car around and headed out to Samantha's place.

When he pulled into her drive, he was relieved to see a light downstairs in the old farmhouse. It was difficult enough involving her in a personal problem without rousting her out of bed in the process. As he crossed the yard and climbed the steps, he failed to see Rory's bike anywhere.

"No need to knock. I'm over here." Samantha's voice came unexpectedly from the far end of the porch. "Is something wrong, Sheriff?" Wrapped in a sweater, she was curled up on the porch swing, nursing a cup of tea. Looking at her, he suddenly realized how cool the air had gone.

"Have you seen Rory?"

"Not since dinnertime." She rose, then walked toward him out of the shadows, concern written on her face. "What's happened?"

"He sneaked out of the house. I thought there might be something going on with your llamas. Any of them sick? About to calve?"

"They're all healthy. And male." She furrowed her brow and seemed to be thinking. "Maybe Red or Mack know what's going on. I thought I interrupted the three of them this afternoon. Discussing something serious."

"What?"

"I have no idea. Let's go ask Red. Mack's out."

He didn't like hearing that. Didn't want to have to start worrying about his buddy as well as his son.

Samantha seemed to pick up on his thoughts. "It's okay. He's at an AA meeting. Sometimes he doubles up." She headed down the porch steps.

Garrett followed. "You don't have to come. I can take it from here."

"Nonsense. Heads together, and all that. Let's check the barn on the way. Has Rory run away before?"

"No." But he'd never been twelve-almost-thirteen before.

"He seems like such a levelheaded kid," she said, stepping into the barn and switching on the lights to reveal gleaming tack and organized containers of food. "Just look at this place. It was never so organized before and Rory's been responsible for all of this. I wonder what got into him tonight."

So did Garrett, but he couldn't help feeling pride despite his concern. Pride at his son's diligence. "Rory?" he called out. "You here?"

When they looked in all the unused stalls and found nothing, Samantha cut the lights. No sooner had they left the barn than they were met by Red hurrying down the hill. "What's going on, Sheriff?"

"Rory's gone missing. You have any idea where he might have headed?"

"Damn." Stopping in front of them, Red glanced guiltily at Samantha. "We didn't want to involve you, Duchess. And I sure didn't think the kid would take matters into his own hands."

"What are you talking about?" Samantha looked as confused as Garrett felt.

"Mack, Rory and me think someone's trying to sabotage your business."

"Sabotage my business? What are you talking about?"

"Stupid stuff. Starting with the garbage in the pasture. Some fence damage. Signs pulled down around town. Juvenile crap but a pain in the butt nonetheless."

"Who would want to upset my little operation?" Samantha folded her arms and hugged them to her chest as if stifling a shiver. "Do you really think it's more than just random acts?"

"Maybe. Maybe not." Red scowled. "I think I know who could be behind it, but I got no proof."

Garrett could guess the culprit, too. Tanner. If for

no other reason than he'd want to jerk Samantha's chain because she'd cut off his ATV access. "But how does this involve Rory tonight?"

"Most of the stuff has taken place after dark. Rory suggested spying on Tanner and his sons. It wasn't a bad idea, but Mack and me told him to leave it to us."

"If he's acting lookout," Samantha said, "I know where he is. The old apple orchard that runs right up along the line by Tanner's house."

"Bingo!" Red headed for his truck. "You two head across the meadow. No lights and no callin' out, though. We don't want Tanner or his boys discovering Rory. Who knows how they'd make his life miserable for the rest of the summer."

"Where are you going?" Garrett asked.

"I'm the decoy. I'll drive right up to Tanner's. Say I'm looking for some tools I think they mighta borrowed."

"But it's after ten."

"Hell, they reckon I'm half-senile as is. They won't think anything's out of the ordinary." The old man took off, looking almost gleeful. As if he were playing out some scene from a rural *Mission: Impossible.*

Garrett began to doubt the wisdom of letting Rory spend his days hanging out with this crew.

"Come on," Samantha said, sensing some unspoken antagonism in Garrett. "Let's go look for your son."

"You don't need to come. Especially if Tanner's involved."

"Oh, yes, I do. It's my property. And my employee. I feel responsible." She headed around the far side of the barn toward the outer pasture. The moon hadn't risen yet, making it difficult to see what was underfoot.

"We're not going to run into those animals of yours, are we?" he asked as she let them through the gate.

"No. They're secured in the inner pasture. Besides, they're not aggressive."

"If you say so."

"I'm getting the feeling you're not keen on this plan. Is there some department procedure you'd rather we followed?"

"I'm here as a father, not the sheriff."

Aha, she thought. *And there lies the problem. You don't want me in the middle of your personal business.* Her irritation quickly dissipated when she realized she'd feel the same in his shoes. "I understand—"

"No talking. Red was right. We don't want Tanner to know Rory was ever near his property. If that's actually where he is."

Okay. She needed to concentrate on her own feet, anyway. Tall grass and rocky hummocks made the going rough as they climbed the rise that led to the orchard. The stars in the moonless sky seemed to hang low overhead, but shed no light. An owl hooted nearby. The scent of honeysuckle drenched the air.

She stumbled twice. Although he was but a few steps away, Garrett didn't reach out to help her. She got the feeling he was angry—but at his son for this adolescent stunt or at her? She didn't get it. Didn't get him.

They were coming to the crest of the rise. She could tell because the breeze kicked up. The old apple orchard was over the hill, then below in a sheltered hollow.

With a screech something passed overhead, so close Samantha could feel the beat of wings. The thought of an owl's sharp talons drove her to her knees, stifling a cry. Seconds later she was hauled to her feet.

"Dammit, you'll get us shot," he hissed, grasping her wrist and pulling her down the hill into the sweet-smelling dell and off the skyline.

When the first of the two dozen apple trees that Red's grandfather had planted appeared as ghostly shadows, Garrett stopped abruptly, causing her to slam into him. He gripped her shoulders, then leaned close to her ear. For a moment she became disoriented in the dark—disoriented by his sheer bulk, the warmth of his cheek, his masculine scent—and only heard part of his rasped command. Something about staying close. When he moved away, she reached out for him. He grabbed her wrist again and pulled her along as if she were some suspect in his custody. She tried to catch her breath.

There were only three rows of trees—the narrow valley wasn't wide enough for more—and Garrett headed for the line closest to the fenced boundary. She could see the back of Tanner's ramshackle house, silhouetted by what must be the porch light out front. Red's truck was nowhere to be seen, but the faint sound of men's voices drifted on the night air.

Garrett headed for the tree that would afford the best view of the Harris's yard. When the dogs started barking—were they chained or loose?—Samantha felt him stiffen, although he didn't slow his pace through the tangled undergrowth. It surprised her that, for such a large man, he moved easily and with almost no noise.

The old trees were gnarled and low, with some of the branches scraping the ground. Easy for a kid to climb. But difficult to maneuver around. Garrett stopped. She could sense him listening. The moon began to show itself above the crest of the rise. Not good. More light upped the chances of discovery. She inhaled sharply. Pressing his hand over her mouth, he pulled her hard up against him at the same time he reached for what looked like a dead branch hanging from the tree.

The "branch" turned out to be a leg, the leg

attached to Rory, who dropped with a thud from above. In an instant, Garrett let Samantha go and was on his son, covering the boy's mouth as he'd done hers. Although no one had spoken, the dogs—free and running behind the boundary fence not twenty feet away—sensed their presence and renewed their baying.

Silhouetted human forms rounded the house. "Whatya got there, boys?" Tanner's voice rang out loud and cheerfully menacing. "Mountain lion? I'll take care of 'im."

"Leave it be!" That had to be Red. "There's too many dogs for it to come closer."

A shotgun blast shattered the night air.

"Stay low," Garrett growled as he crouched and hauled both Rory and Samantha behind him. "And run."

He cut a path, not up to the ridgeline where they'd be outlined in the moonlight, but into the trees then down the hollow that abutted Tanner's property. Although they were concealed, the dogs knew where they were and ran the length of the fence in a frenzy while raucous male laughter trailed them. Samantha felt her heart might burst from her chest.

As the dell widened into the lower pasture, they were still a long way from the farmhouse. Garrett pulled them toward the fence that ran along the county road, where headlights bobbled crazily toward them. "That'll be Red."

"How do you know—?"

"Hush."

"Dad, hold up!" These were the first words Rory had spoken.

"Not before we clear the fence." Garrett practically tossed his son over, and for the first time Samantha could see the boy was weighted down by binoculars around his neck and a backpack that now hung by one strap from his shoulder.

Garrett turned to her, but she'd already decided she wasn't going to be pitched like a sack of feed. She clambered over the rail just as Red pulled his pickup to a stop on the road's shoulder.

Without being told, Rory climbed into the truck bed, followed by Samantha, then Garrett. Red took off before the three had a chance to settle in, and Samantha slid the length of the gravelly bed on her thigh, coming to a stop only as she slammed into Garrett. Despite her sturdy khaki hiking pants, she'd have one enormous road rash come morning.

"Do you think you and your llamas are worth all this?" he snapped as she tried to extricate herself from his grasp.

Even if she weren't bruised and shaken, she wouldn't have attempted to explain to him that she had nothing to do with the night's excitement. His face in the moonlight told her he wasn't in any mood to listen. Instead, she crawled toward the cab, where Rory was slumped against a bale of hay. "You okay?" she asked.

He nodded but didn't look at her. He and his father seemed locked in a glaring match.

Red came to a halt in front of her house. "I don't know about y'all," he said as the three piled out of the back of his truck, "but I could use a drink. Sorry, Duchess, but that's the truth."

"Another time." Garrett clapped a hand on Rory's shoulder and propelled him to the cruiser.

"Is he going to catch hell from his father?" Samantha asked Red as she watched them drive away. She had a sudden urge for a drink as well, and knew she'd be calling her sponsor as soon as Red left.

"Catch hell? You bet. But nothing physical, don't worry on that score. Garrett's not that kind of a pa."

"Can you tell me what's going on? Why would Rory pull such a stunt?"

"The kid was just trying on his shining armor." When Samantha shot him a thoroughly confused look, Red added, "You hadn't noticed in addition to really digging those llamas, Rory's got a huge crush on you?"

She sighed deeply. This was not the small town involvement she'd envisioned.

GARRETT DIDN'T WAIT TO GET home to begin the interrogation. "Please, explain to me why you were in a tree outside Tanner Harris's house. In the dark." Hands gripping the steering wheel, he shot a glance at his son's chest. "With my night binoculars."

Rory didn't answer.

"Red already said you and he and Mack suspected Tanner had been vandalizing Whistling Meadows. Why didn't you talk to me?"

"Because we didn't have proof," Rory mumbled.

"So you thought you'd take the law in your own hands and run a stakeout."

"To get proof, yeah. I was going to get a picture with my phone and e-mail it to your office."

"Did you not take one second to consider who you're dealing with? Tanner Harris. Almost every resident in this county owns a gun, yes, but Tanner has an arsenal. As you saw tonight, he doesn't hesitate to shoot first and ask questions never. You could have been killed."

Pain squeezed Garrett's chest. This wasn't some juvenile delinquent he was trying to scare straight. This was his son, and he didn't want to think about how close he'd come to tragedy.

"Whatever possessed you to do this yourself?" he continued in an effort to regain a semblance of control. "Samantha Weston is an adult." He thought about how determined she was to be right in the thick of things—tonight and with Mack a week ago. Why? Was she one of those women who had to have men falling all over themselves in her wake? "Looks like she can take care of her own affairs."

"Red says looks can be deceiving. Says we need to watch out for her."

"Rory, you're being paid minimum wage to help with the llamas. You're not Samantha Weston's security guard."

"I was helping with the llamas, Dad. Red says Tanner doesn't treat his dogs like living creatures but like property. Don't you see what an easy step it would be from vandalizing Samantha's property to hurting the llamas?"

"She needs to file a complaint with the depart-ment, then." He pulled into their driveway. "And you need to find another job. One where you're not stuck in the middle of a brewing feud."

"You can't be serious." Rory's whole body lan-guage changed. From a scared kid huddling in the corner to a feisty bantamweight boxer itching to get in the ring and fight.

"I'm stone-cold serious." His son might feel mature enough to take on his father, but he had to understand who was still in charge. Garrett clutched the wheel and looked right into Rory's eyes. "I'll drive up to Whistling Meadows tomorrow to explain why you won't be coming back to work."

Rory was the first to look away. "You're the one who's always saying, 'Don't be a quitter.'" His voice cracked with emotion.

"This is different, son. This situation could turn ugly. And dangerous." And this was his only child.

"You're ruining my life!" Rory shouted as he hurtled from the car and escaped into the house.

Garrett's cell phone rang. It was Noelle. "Where's Rory?"

"We just got home. He's…in the shower."

"Why hasn't he answered my messages?"

"Noelle, this is Applegate. Life's a little more un-plugged here."

"I was worried about him."

"Don't be. He's fine." At least he would be as soon as Garrett pulled in a few favors to find his son a job away from Whistling Meadows.

CHAPTER SIX

WHO KNEW HE'D HAVE TO MAKE an appointment with Samantha to talk about his son?

Earlier in the morning when Garrett had driven Rory to Whistling Meadows—Rory had insisted he wasn't going to leave Samantha high and dry without advance notice, and, as he cooled down, Garrett could see his point—he'd found Samantha gone. To AA with Mack. Rory had looked at the schedule that hung in the barn, which indicated that when she got back she had a lunch trek with the Optimist Club from Sapphire Lake. While she was out, he and Red were going to clear some brush from the inner pasture. Shouldering heavy pruning equipment, his son shot Garrett a look that brooked no argument. As if to say Rory was a man, and that was that.

Garrett had watched him walk away and reminded himself that, for all the swagger, he was still a twelve-year-old boy. His son. Who could have taken some buckshot last night. For a woman who had no connection to them.

What was this hold she had over not only Rory, but Red and Mack as well?

He'd called the Whistling Meadows business number and left a message that he'd be back at four that afternoon and would appreciate it if Samantha cleared fifteen minutes of time to discuss a matter of importance.

Now five-to-four, he drove up her rutted drive to see her leaning on the pasture fence, feeding a carrot to one of the llamas. Farther up the hill, Rory, Red and Mack sat on the bunkhouse porch, elbows on knees, staring at him. They looked a little like avenging angels. Or gargoyles. Or Hear-No-Evil, See-No-Evil, Speak-No-Evil. Whatever. They didn't appear to be on his side.

Wiping her hands on her jeans, Samantha came to meet him as he stepped out of the cruiser. Dressed in a T-shirt, covered by an ordinary flannel shirt, she seemed a little less designer today, a little more country. As if she'd taken serious root in Applegate. "Rory says you don't want him working for me anymore," she said without preamble. "That's a little harsh, don't you think?"

"You were there. You didn't hear the gunshot?"

"Red and I've talked to Rory already," she countered. "He understands that what he did was reckless. Way beyond his job description. He's promised to discuss any concerns he has in the future about Whistling Meadows with me. As has Red." There was an imperiousness to her tone of voice that rubbed him the wrong way. She might have traded the designer-casual look for work clothes, but her manner said she was no naive farmer's daughter.

"You're saying you knew nothing about this little scheme," he said, unable to keep the disbelief from tightening his words.

"That's what I'm saying. And I knew nothing about any of the problems—except for the garbage. I saw that. For some reason both Red and Rory thought they were being gallant, keeping me in the dark."

"So you admit there's an issue with Tanner Harris."

"Perhaps. Then again, the incidences could be unrelated. The result of kids with not enough to keep them occupied."

"But if another situation arises, you'll contact me instead of sending out your private posse."

"I repeat. I didn't instruct them to take on my battles."

Okay. If they were going to have a spitting contest, he was ready. "*I repeat.* If you have any more problems, you need to contact me. Or someone in the department."

She visibly bristled, tossing her curls and tilting her chin so that when she looked at him, he got the impression she was looking down her nose even though she was a head shorter than he was. "I can handle Mr. Harris," she said defiantly.

"Don't handle him alone. You're not from around here. You don't understand the dynamics of boundaries and perceived insult and long memories."

"But I haven't done anything wrong." She glanced over her shoulder toward the rise and Tanner's property beyond. "I bought Whistling Meadows fair and square. The Harrises are going to have to get used to the fact it's not their private park anymore."

"It's wiser to let the law handle some things."

He sensed she was ready with a sharp retort, then thought better of it.

"Look, I don't have anything against you managing your own operation," he said, "but I grew up with Tanner Harris. He's a sneak. If he's out to get you, you're not going to see him coming. As sheriff, I'm here to protect your interests. As a father, I'm here to protect my son's. I don't want him in the middle of a feud."

"You're saying just working for me puts him in danger?"

"I can't take that chance."

"I think he's safe. There are, after all, three adults living here."

Now there was a whole other topic of conversation.

"Besides, I've come to depend on Rory," she insisted. "If you make him quit, I'm left shorthanded just as my business is taking off."

"You got along without him for three months. You can manage till you find a replacement. Which won't be hard. In case you hadn't noticed, summer jobs for kids are at a premium around here."

"I know. I already held interviews. And out of all the applicants, I chose Rory."

Not liking her proprietary air, Garrett set his jaw.

"You're not going to budge on this, are you?" she asked. "I think you're being unreasonable. Your son's not a baby. Besides, there's risk everywhere. What if you sent him to one of the local camps and he got thrown from a horse, gouged with a piece of wood-working equipment, flipped on a whitewater rafting expedition—"

"I get your point." When he saw his hard-ass stance wasn't swaying her, he adopted a different approach. "You're a woman. Surely you can see Rory's mother's perspective. She sends our kid to me for the summer and expects—quite reasonably—to get him back in one piece."

"You're patronizing me."

"No. I'm trying to be honest, but this conversation's finished." He turned to look up the hill where the three gargoyles were still perched. Still staring him down. "Rory, come on! We're leaving."

"Red'll give me a ride," his son shouted back, not moving.

He didn't have time for an additional confrontation. Rory could get a lift with Red, if he wanted, but he wasn't coming back to work for Samantha. It was as simple as that. Garrett got in the cruiser and drove deliberately off her property and onto the county road. And then the most amazing thing happened. He looked in his rearview mirror to see a crazy woman on a bicycle following him. Pedaling as if she meant to run him down.

With every rotation of the pedals, Samantha grew angrier and angrier. She'd been ready to discuss last night's incident, to discuss how Garrett and she could each reinforce with Rory that his gallantry was not to be repeated. But she hadn't been prepared to be lectured like some miscreant. Some irresponsible, or worse yet, manipulative employer. Or, most insulting of all, some stupidly helpless female who needed Mr. I-Run-This-County to step in and organize her business. Or her life.

Besides, she didn't buy Garrett McQuire's omnipotent veneer.

Fuming, she nearly ran into the back of the car, which had now stopped. The sheriff leaned out the window. "Is there some reason you're tailgating me?" The crinkles at the corners of his sharp blue eyes told her he was trying hard not to laugh.

Well, this was no laughing matter.

She pulled up beside the car. "I don't believe we came to any resolution back there."

He sighed—actually had the unmitigated gall to sigh. "We can't come to it here. The road's too narrow. There's a school bus turnaround just past Tanner's drive. I'll pull in there." He looked at her bike. "Try not to get killed."

"Thank you very much, but I'm still alive after three months of negotiating these roads," she muttered as she followed the cruiser.

He pulled in, stopped, then turned on the car's flashing lights before stepping out.

"Is that really necessary?" she asked, scowling at the display.

"Yes," he replied without explanation.

Ah—this man didn't want any passing motorist to think he had anything but official business with her. She had a sudden insight that curved right back to the issue with Rory. Garrett, for whatever reason, wanted to be seen as by the book, unassailably right and in control.

"I think you used the excuse of Rory's mother as a smoke screen back there."

"What the hell are you talking about?"

"To cover your own fears."

"My fears?"

"Yes. I can see it in your eyes. You're afraid of losing Rory. Whether to—God forbid!—a tragedy, or to your ex-wife, or to adulthood. You're afraid of all the things parents have to be afraid of…but, most of all, you're afraid to admit your fears."

The expression on his face was as if she'd punched him in the solar plexus.

"Plus, you don't want to let anyone else help you with the transitions that will naturally occur in your son's life. People like Red or me."

"So you're not only a llama handler, but you're a shrink?" Half of his upper lip twitched. "Excuse me if I'm not impressed."

A car drove by. The driver waved and tooted his horn. The sheriff narrowed his eyes.

"I'm not asking you to be impressed," she said. "I'm asking you to let go the parental reins a little and allow Rory to continue working for me. Red and I will take good care of him, I promise. And if it even looks as if we weren't, there'd be hell to pay in the form of Mack."

"Lady, I have to ask you what you put in your drinking water to have three males falling all over themselves for your benefit."

"I let them know I saw their fear, and I wasn't

judging. I've been there, too. I've come through to a better place."

Garrett took a step back as if she were bewitched. "There isn't a frightened bone in Red Harris's body—"

"He was afraid of losing his land. Afraid of growing old alone. Your son is afraid of disappointing you. As is M—" She stopped abruptly. She'd said too much.

"What about Mack?"

"He made me promise I wouldn't discuss him or his business."

"I'm his best friend." She saw deep hurt in his gaze.

"I know." She also realized he was scared of losing that friendship. "I wish I could offer you an explanation, but a promise is a promise."

She understood then, by the hardening of his features, that she'd made a grave misstep. If she wouldn't give on Mack, he wouldn't give on Rory.

"I don't make decisions because I'm afraid," he said, looking her right in the eye. "I make decisions because I'm the adult in charge. Of my son's welfare. Today's his last day at Whistling Meadows." Breaking eye contact, he got in the cruiser and drove away, lights still flashing.

What was it about the man that made him so inflexible? And that got under her skin?

Red had told her about Garrett's foster home upbringing. Had told her, too, about how his wife had left him for more opportunity than she felt a small town could provide. But was that the whole of what made him tick?

And why did she care?

Maybe because he reminded her just the tiniest bit of her father. The steamroller in a tux. The steamroller part was oh so similar, only with Garrett the tux had been replaced with a starched uniform, a Stetson and a sexy pair of aviator sunglasses.

Had she just used the word *sexy* to describe Garrett McQuire? Was the sun getting to her?

"You have a little dustup with the sheriff?"

Samantha whirled around to find herself face-to-face with Tanner Harris, who leered at her rather menacingly as he leaned on the mailbox at the end of his drive. Had he been watching? And waiting for the sheriff to leave? The thought made her shiver.

"A dustup? Not at all," she lied, rubbing her arms. "He wanted to know if the llamas would march in the July Fourth parade."

Tanner narrowed his eyes, and Samantha could almost see the cogs in his brain turning slowly as he wondered whether to believe her.

"Speaking of llamas," she said, seizing the opportunity to catch him off balance by throwing a second idea on top of the first. "I've been having a little trouble, and I wanted to get your opinion on the matter. I think neighbors should stick together, don't you?"

"What kind of trouble?"

"Just a few minor incidences. I don't even know if they're related. It started with the garbage in the pasture near the road…"

As she listed the petty acts of vandalism, she watched Tanner's face. He didn't look at her, and while she recounted her "little troubles" in a very matter-of-fact tone of voice, he fidgeted. Typical bully, brave until confronted.

"I just wondered if you'd heard any rumors," she said sweetly, "that might make sense of all this."

"Can't say as I have."

"Well, if you do—" she drew one of her business cards out of her pocket and handed it to him "—please, give me a call. And you can let it be known round town that I'm here to stay."

He scowled at her card. "You got a gun?"

"Why do you ask?"

"Last night I scared some varmint off our boundary. Coyote, maybe. Possibly bear. Or mountain lion. Didn't get a good look. Those llamas of yours are nothin' more than sittin' ducks."

Was that a threat? Even if it weren't, this was the second suggestion to arm herself for the safety of her livestock. Although coming into this operation, she knew llamas were often used to protect sheep, she needed to do more research on what, short of firearms and beyond vigilance and sturdy fences, was necessary to protect her small herd.

"I appreciate your concern," she said, getting on her bicycle.

"Well, would you look at that!" Tanner's attention had turned from her to a spot beneath them where the road snaked in hairpin turns up the steep hill from town. A sleek black limo, its polished grill glinting in the sun, was making its slow ascent. "Who d'ya suppose is traveling in style?"

Samantha knew, and knowing, wished she had a stiff drink.

CHAPTER SEVEN

PEDALING HER BICYCLE WITH A profound resignation,
Samantha felt the draft from the limo as it passed her
on the way to Whistling Meadows. It didn't stop.
There was no reason for it to. Even if they'd discovered her location, her parents wouldn't expect her to
be traveling the byways by bicycle. They'd expect
her to cope with her loss of license by hiring a chauffeur wherever she might settle.

When the limo turned into the farm lane, it slowed
considerably, the driver apparently having difficulty
maneuvering the car's low-slung chassis over the
ruts and rocks. By the time it came to a halt before
the farmhouse, Samantha had nearly caught up. The
driver's door opened, and Ruggiero got out. He
looked with disdain at "his baby's" surface now
covered with a film of dust before opening the rear
door and offering his hand to Samantha's mother.

Helena Lawrence appeared from the backseat as
gracefully as a butterfly emerging from its cocoon.

As if in slow motion, she pressed her hands to her chest and turned to take in her surroundings. When she caught sight of Samantha pedaling toward her, her face broke into a brilliant smile. "Darling!" She opened wide her arms and waited for her only child to come to her.

Samantha dropped the bicycle in the middle of the yard and strode toward Helena. "Mother, I'm not sure you want that embrace." She looked at her mother's spotless white linen trousers, her pale apricot silk shell, then at her own soiled and sweaty work clothes.

Her mother bent ever so slightly forward to air kiss both of Samantha's cheeks. "What have you been up to, silly girl?"

Cameron Lawrence's head, with its mane of white hair, appeared over the top of the limo. "Ashley, is this some kind of a joke?"

"Dad. What a surprise." *Not.*

Her father came around the car to envelope her in a bear hug while Ruggiero began to buff the limo with a chamois he'd retrieved from the trunk.

When she finally caught her breath, Samantha looked over her shoulder toward the road. "Did anyone follow you?" The last thing she needed was a media circus led by her chauffeured parents.

"No!" Cameron's subsequent laugh exploded

across the barnyard. "Your mother should be a writer. Intrigue suits her. Helena, it's your story…"

"Oh, my, we had fun." Her mother's hands fluttered in the air. "Well, we knew the press was still interested in your…situation, so I cooked up a little scheme to foil them—"

Samantha sighed. "Little schemes" were her mother's stock in trade.

"Don't you worry, darling," Helena cooed. "This is truly marvelous. But, please, get me out of the sun for the telling. I'm parched beyond words."

Samantha glanced at her watch. Five o'clock. Afternoon teatime at any of the Ashley hotels. She might be able to scrounge a few Earl Grey bags and some Oreo cookies from her farmhouse pantry. "Come inside," she offered without enthusiasm. "I'll see what I can provide by way of refreshment."

Her parents glanced at each other.

"And you can tell me your story." She indicated the porch. "Please."

As Helena and Cameron gingerly mounted the steps, Samantha noted with dismay the third tread from the bottom needed nailing down. She also noted—with relief—that Red's truck was gone. He must have driven Rory home. She needed time to prepare herself, let alone the rest of Applegate, for her parents' visit.

Holding the front door open, she saw the interior of the farmhouse for the first time as though through someone else's eyes. The living room was empty. She was so happily tired by the end of each day the only lounging she did was in bed for maybe three minutes before she fell soundly asleep. If she sat at all it was on the porch swing, listening to the night noises. While Red had taken the kitchen table, he'd left her the big dining room trestle table that seated twelve. And that was the entirety of her furniture on the first floor. Her real life took place beyond these walls.

Her father said nothing, but after a stunned silence, her mother said, "This may have been a brilliant decision…to start with a blank canvas."

Samantha propelled her parents to the table. "Have a seat."

Her mother looked about dubiously. "There are no screens on the windows."

"I haven't gotten around to putting them up yet. But the citronella geraniums on the sill deter the bugs. Relax. Enjoy the view."

Her father pulled a chair out for her mother as Samantha suddenly remembered a basket of raspberries she'd picked from the ancient canes that circled the kitchen garden. And the homemade pimento cheese sandwiches, granola cookies and fabulous peach iced tea Rachel had sent as a sample of some of the things the diner might provide if Samantha decided to have box lunches catered for special treks. A feast! With a light heart she left her parents for the kitchen. She reminded herself not to apologize for her surroundings or her cuisine. Or her decision to stay in Applegate.

"Go on with your story," she said, head and shoulders in the fridge. "About not being followed. I can hear you."

"Ah, yes, back to eluding the noxious paparazzi." From the dining room her mother's voice tinkled like a wind chime. "Do you remember Bitsy Cross? People say we could be sisters. I let it be known I was going to the West Coast for a little cosmetic touch-up and that Bitsy would be accompanying me for moral support. Daddy announced he'd be meeting with suppliers in Romania—"

Samantha searched her cupboards in vain for tea-worthy dishes, then stopped herself. She wasn't on display. She'd get out the locally made blue pottery she used daily.

"Well, Bitsy and I headed for California," Helena continued, "where she, disguised in my clothes—a lovely de la Renta outfit—and a huge scarf and dark glasses, checked into Dr. Wheaton's clinic. As me. Well, as me under an assumed name. She's actually going to have a tummy tuck—"

"Mother! Back to the press, please," Samantha urged as she arranged food on plates.

"This is all part of the story, darling! As soon as Bitsy was settled in, I flew to the Ipswiches' home in West Palm, where Ruggerio was waiting. I think he took a bus. Your father arrived a couple days later, then we borrowed the Ipswiches' limo—I'm surprised you didn't notice it wasn't one of our fleet— and drove north from Florida. And, voilà! Here we are. Without benefit of the media."

Samantha's heart sank.

"You don't look pleased," her father said as he appeared in the kitchen doorway.

"Oh, Dad. Would you convince Mother not to repeat that story?"

"Why not? It's funny."

Perhaps. But with its convoluted plot and gratuitous expenses, it was so far removed from everyday life in Applegate that people—Garrett sprang to mind—would look at her parents—and her, by association—as if the Lawrences had dropped in from Mars. Her parents would be leaving. Hopefully, soon. But Samantha intended to stay. And not as some alien.

"Ah-h-h!" Helena's high-pitched scream sliced the air.

Samantha and her father rushed into the dining room to see her mother backed up against the wall as Percy's head and neck, framed by two geranium pots, stretched toward the seat where Helena had just been sitting.

TEN O'CLOCK THAT NIGHT Garrett was in the parking lot behind headquarters, filling emergency sandbags by lamplight. Sampson's Creek ran behind the buildings on Main Street and was known to overflow with a heavy rain. Enough that the businesses on this side of Main kept ready piles of sand, shovels and burlap sacks. Not that it had rained recently or that there was any forecast soon. Garrett simply needed some mindless physical labor to take his thoughts off his personal business.

Rory.

For the first time ever Rory was giving Garrett the silent treatment. Because Garrett had told him he couldn't keep the job at Whistling Meadows.

"You need help?" The voice was startling in its familiarity. Mack.

Garrett turned to see his friend clean and apparently sober. Even so, that old devilish glint in his eyes was gone, replaced by…nothing.

"I never turn down an offer of help," Garrett said, tossing Mack a shovel.

"That's not what I hear."

Damn. Was this a lecture coming?

"Okay, tell me what people are saying." Both men began to shovel and bag. It was as good excuse as any to avoid eye contact.

"My godson's mighty pissed you pulled him off the job," Mack said at last. "And Red's not so happy you won't let him and Samantha work with you to sort Rory out. As if he were a bonafide employee and young adult and not some shrinking violet that needs the hothouse treatment."

"You think I'm overprotecting him?"

"Hell, yeah. Don't you remember the scrapes we were getting in when we were his age?"

Did he ever. Garrett found himself smiling at the thought of "borrowing" Jeb Whittaker's ancient farm truck—the one that wasn't even registered—to drive to the movies to sit behind Liz Humphreys and Caitlin Ford. They had been all thirteen at the time. Just about Rory's age.

"You're thinking about that old truck, aren't you?" Mack asked.

"Yeah." That night at the movies wasn't the only time they used it. Garrett thought about the hairpin turns on the local roads. "God, we could have been killed."

"But we weren't."

Garrett looked at his friend. "Why was it no big deal then when I was actually going through it, and now…just the thought of my son in harm's way makes me feel sick?"

A shade seemed to drop down over Mack's features. "I don't know." He stuck his shovel in the pile of sand with a violent stabbing motion. "I gotta get going. But I wanted to ask you to give Rory another chance."

"Even if I wanted Rory to keep his job at Whistling Meadows, there's something about the Weston woman that makes me uneasy."

"Samantha?" Mack looked dumbfounded. "Man, she's a stand-up individual. Salt of the earth. You have no worries where she's concerned. She'll do right by Rory." He turned to go. "Don't be so quick to judge. Be more a man and less a sheriff."

"You need a ride back to Red's?" Garrett asked, looking for a way to change the subject.

"No, thanks. My sponsor's picking me up. Driving still makes me jumpy. And nights are trouble."

Garrett had to ask. "Are you seeing your way to come back to the department?"

"Sorry, but I can't plan that far ahead. I'm having trouble figuring out fifteen minutes at a time." Without looking back, Mack disappeared around the corner of the building, leaving Garrett with a small mountain of excess sandbags and the incessant mournful cry of the whip-poor-will.

He'd better head home, although he still hadn't decided whether to cave to the entreaties about Rory's job. Hell, if he let his son back on that farm, he'd just have to keep a sharper eye on Tanner's activities.

His cell phone chirped. "Hello?"

"It's Noelle. I forgot to ask you what you thought Rory might like for his birthday."

He'd totally forgotten Rory was going to be thirteen next Monday.

"I'm going to try to get away to celebrate with the two of you," Noelle continued, seemingly without taking a breath, "but I made it to the second round for that promotion. I may need to fly back to London next week. So if I can't be in Applegate, Rory's present has to be awesome. Any ideas?"

"I'll do some probing and get back to you."

"Money's no object," she said, and Garrett could hear the smug satisfaction in her voice.

"I'll see what I can do," he replied, signing off and reminding himself Rory's upcoming birthday was a passage in their son's life. Not a competition.

Any therapeutic benefits of an hour's worth of shifting sand had worn off in one brief conversation. He needed a hot shower and a good night's sleep. He stuck his shovel next to Mack's.

Rounding the corner onto Main, he automatically did a visual check. At this end of the street, the Laundromat was still open—two men were playing checkers on a bench inside as their clothes tumbled in dryers—as was the liquor store. Nothing out of the ordinary there. But parked in front of the liquor store was a big black limo. Not a stretch, but definitely a limo. With a uniformed chauffeur standing outside the driver's door. In a minute a young woman stepped out of the store, wine bottle in hand. She seemed to hesitate. The chauffeur, who was facing the street, didn't notice her immediately.

But Garrett sure did.

There was no denying this woman was the limo's passenger. Sophisticated and beautiful, she wore a strapless black dress. Elegant and sexy at the same time. Her blond hair was swept high on her head, leaving a pale neck and shoulders that gleamed satiny smooth in the lamplight. And because she looked so out of place on Applegate's Main Street, as if she'd been dropped from the sky, she took Garrett's breath away.

When she glanced across the street and caught his eye, he couldn't believe she was—

"Samantha?"

The chauffeur turned toward her, then rounded the hood to open the passenger door.

With a startled look on her face, she whipped the wine bottle behind her back. Maybe Garrett was a fool for interfering, but there were too many people—three males in particular—who trusted this woman. "Samantha, wait!"

He crossed the street to confront her.

The chauffeur discreetly returned to the driver's side of the car.

"Garrett…hello." She suddenly appeared less like a woman of the world and more like a kid with her hand caught in the cookie jar.

He reached around her to take the wine bottle out of her grasp. "You don't want to do this."

"Oh, I do." Her shoulders slumped. "I do, I do, I do."

What had happened since four o'clock that afternoon?

Samantha looked at Garrett and tried hard not to cry. He was the last person she wanted to see her backslide. The wine was the topper, but the rest was equally embarrassing. The use of her father's limo, her mother's dress. The return of the woman who, to keep the peace, had transformed herself into the dutiful daughter for an evening. The dutiful, unhappy daughter.

"What's wrong?" Garrett's voice was low and full of concern. Lacking any of the macho bluster of this afternoon. "Where are you going?"

"Where have I been, you mean." In the borrowed strappy sandals, she kicked at a sidewalk planter filled with geraniums. "I've been to hell. Camouflaged as the Grove Park Inn's formal dining room."

"Who's this guy?" Garrett cocked his head toward Ruggiero. "Does he turn into a mouse at midnight?"

She forced a smile. "My parents' chauffeur. They're staying at the inn. Ruggiero's driving me home."

"Were you planning to drink this?" Garrett held up the bottle.

"Most definitely."

"Why didn't you call your sponsor?"

"That sounds so easy." He couldn't know how much she wanted that wine. "It's not."

"Then you're stuck with me. Let's find somewhere we can talk." As he looked around the last of the storefronts on the street went dark.

Ruggiero, his back still to them, cleared his throat.

"We can talk in the limo," she said. "Ruggiero will drive me home, then you." She tried to think of how angry she'd been with Garrett that afternoon. Over Rory. But that was before her past had shown up. Now she only felt vulnerable. "I could use the company."

Ruggiero walked around the car, opened the door, then handed her into the seat. He stepped aside and waited for Garrett to follow her. Settled in the back, Samantha made certain the soundproof partition was closed. If she was going to vent—and she most certainly was going to—she didn't want her parents' loyal employee carrying tales.

Feeling the powerful purr of the limo's engine as Ruggiero pulled onto Main Street and headed toward Whistling Meadows, she kicked off the uncomfortable spike-heeled sandals. The heady aroma of leather and of the fresh-cut flowers in small sconces next to the windows pulled her into a world that seemed foreign to her now. Even stranger was the presence of the man beside her. Talk about a heady experience. Although his presence filled the darkened interior of the luxury car, he sat quietly next to her, his knee touching hers, his demeanor one of discomfort.

"Can I get you something to drink?" she asked, automatically falling into hostess mode. "Mother made sure the bar was stripped of alcoholic beverages, but there's soda."

"Forget the drinks," he said, looking straight at her. "Tell me what has you so upset?"

"My parents. Now doesn't that sound ungrateful?" Remembering that he'd been brought up in foster homes, she mentally kicked herself. "Let me start again. I love them both dearly. But I can't play the role they've designed for me."

"I take it they don't want you running llama treks in Applegate, North Carolina."

She rolled her eyes to indicate the limo. "You think?"

"Hey, it could be a rental." There was the hint of a smile in his eyes.

"Well, it isn't a rental." Borrowed didn't count when the Lawrences' own fleet included a dozen or more. She threw her head back against the cushioned seat. "I'm never going to survive their being here!"

"Tell yourself it's just a visit. How long are they planning on staying?"

"Oh!" she wailed, "for as long as it takes to complete their projects."

"Projects?"

"Mother can't wait to decorate the farmhouse. Can you say 'extreme makeover'? And Daddy always likes to look for large tracts of land—"

She saw Garrett's eyebrows jut skyward and realized she'd said too much. Earlier she'd made her parents promise, promise, promise they wouldn't blow her cover. She'd even played the melodrama card and told them if the equanimity she'd achieved in Applegate wasn't maintained, Dr. Kumar feared she'd suffer a relapse. That had frightened them enough that by evening's end they were calling her Samantha.

"I don't want to talk about my parents," she stated emphatically.

"Then let's talk about the bottle of wine you bought." Which lay on the floor between his feet. "Wasn't that just running away from your problems?"

"As fast as I possibly could."

"Do you still want that drink?"

"Yes, please."

"Samantha…" With his foot he drew the bottle up against the seat and out of sight. "How would your sponsor counsel you?"

She sighed. He wasn't going to give her the wine. "She might first suggest a strong diversion." She turned to look at Garrett, whose eyes were trained on her in the most disconcerting way. "Do you happen to have any knitting on you?"

"No…" His gaze was faintly roguish. "Guess we'll have to come up with something else to distract you."

Was he flirting with her?

She looked away to trail the pad of her thumb over the petals in the nearest sconce. "Flower arranging?" she suggested. *Lame, Samantha, really lame.*

She felt his fingertips on her chin. With just the slightest pressure, he turned her face toward his. Seeing undeniable want in his eyes, she realized this wasn't just about her needs anymore.

He was going to kiss her.

He moved so slowly she could have turned away, but that was the last thing she wanted to do at the moment. Call her crazy.

When his lips found hers, she inhaled sharply. He was so warm. How had she ever thought him cold?

When he pulled her up against him, she twined her arms around his neck and gave in to the kiss. It was hot. And sure of itself. And like no other kiss Ashley Lawrence had ever experienced—

But did Garrett want Samantha Weston of the jeans and T-shirts or this dressed-up, false reflection of her past life?

She pulled away just as the limo came to a stop in front of her farmhouse. Without waiting for the chauffeur to open the door, she got out. To Ruggiero she said, "Take the sheriff home."

To Garrett she said, "That wasn't a diversion. That was a potentially dangerous detour." Angry at herself for giving in to the second incautious impulse of the night, she slammed the car door before he could reply.

She was walking a tightrope in her recovery. Hadn't the wine purchase proved the precariousness of her balance? How could she possibly consider romantic involvement, no matter how fleeting? Dr. Kumar had said she needed to learn to love herself before she could consider sharing that love.

Sadly, she watched the limo pull away and realized she wanted that drink more than ever before. Barefoot—she'd left her mother's sandals in the car—she hobbled across the pebble-strewn yard and up the porch steps. To call her sponsor.

CHAPTER EIGHT

GARRETT STOOD ON HIS FRONT steps and watched the retreating taillights of Samantha's limo. What had he told himself only days ago? Ask her out. Prove how unsuited they were for each other. Get over her.

Yeah, right.

So the past half hour hadn't been a date, but it had been enough time to highlight how wrong she was for him. If that big chauffeured car didn't prove it, Samantha's slamming the door in his face did. Now came the hard part—getting over the thought of her.

That wasn't going to happen.

Mack had told him to act more like a man and less like a sheriff. Well, the reaction Garrett had experienced seeing Samantha dressed to kill was miles from sheriff. The kiss had been instinct. So where did acting like a man get him?

Alone on his front steps. Thinking about a woman he couldn't have. Wanting more than that first electrifying kiss.

Puzzled, he ran his fingers through his hair, shook himself back to reality, then entered the house. Rory was watching TV in the living room. "Hey," Garrett said, standing in the doorway.

Rory ignored him.

His interpersonal skills were taking a hit these days. Determined not to let his most important relationship deteriorate, he sat on the opposite end of the sofa from his son. "You can't stay mad at me forever. We need to talk. Let's start with a positive subject. What do you want for your birthday?"

Rory actually looked at him. "I want to keep my job at Whistling Meadows, *and* I want you to take a whole day off Monday."

"I think your mother was thinking of something she could wrap."

Shrugging, his son turned back toward the television screen. "That's all I want."

The job-bargaining chip Garrett might have foreseen, but the request for him to take a whole day off surprised him. He was sheriff and could pretty much arrange his own hours. But right from his election, he'd taken the public trust thing seriously. Because it wasn't so much a job as a commitment, he'd never officially put himself down for a day off on the schedule. Not a day went by when he didn't put on his uniform.

"What do you want to do," he asked, "that would require me to take a whole day off?"

"I want us to go on a llama trek."

"What if your mother can get away from her job? She wants to celebrate with you." He couldn't picture Noelle hiking, let alone hiking with those strange-looking creatures.

"Then she can come along. It's my birthday. It's supposed to be about what I want."

Maybe Noelle was just an excuse. Garrett couldn't picture himself spending a day with the llamas. Or with Samantha.

But this was his son, whom he saw only on vacations. He didn't want to waste the brief time they had together being at odds. Besides, if he were honest with himself, Rory wasn't asking for anything outrageous. "Okay," he said finally.

"Okay, job? Or okay, trek? Or okay, both?"

"Okay, both."

"All right!" Rory pumped the air with his fist, and the smile that split his face was worth the concession. "Wanna play a game of chess?"

"Sure. As soon as you call your mother to tell her what you want for your birthday." Noelle and he could split the trek cost.

LATE THURSDAY AFTERNOON Samantha was trying to conduct business on the phone at the same time she was supposed to be paying attention to her mother, who was shopping—her favorite pastime—in the one antique store in Applegate. They were looking for accessories for Samantha's farmhouse.

When the whole decorating project had been proposed, Samantha had been adamant that she had a business to run, and her mother had agreed to entertain herself mornings and midday while Samantha conducted her scheduled treks. Helena had sighed and said she could spend most of the day at the Grove Park Inn's fabulous spa, but Samantha would absolutely have to promise her late afternoons and evenings. Her father took care of himself. If he didn't have a golf game, he buried himself in the county land office, scouting bargains.

Worrying about her parents' activities was actually preferable to thinking about a drink. Or about the undeniable attraction she'd felt toward Garrett last night.

"Hello…?" The voice at the other end of the line bristled with impatience.

"I'm sorry," Samantha replied. "I don't seem to be getting very good reception. Let me move." With that excuse, she motioned to her mother that she needed to handle this call, then stepped outside the shop. She couldn't muster any enthusiasm for buying old stuff for a farmhouse from which Red had just removed his own family antiques. "Are you still there?" she asked the woman. With all the distractions she hadn't caught the woman's name, if indeed it had been given. "You wanted to schedule a trek?"

"Yes. For my son's birthday."

"How many will be in the party?"

"Just two. My son and his father. I have to fly to London tomorrow on business. Because I won't be there, I want this to be an awesome day. Do you do overnight camping trips?"

"Uh…not usually…" Samantha watched Ruggiero coming out of the antique shop, carrying a small rustic bench. He stowed it in the trunk of the limo beside the boxes of fabric swatches her mother had had overnighted from her interior designer in Virginia. He then went back into the shop. The thought of Helena's decorating plans gave Samantha a headache. Made her want to escape. "But…we might be able to arrange an overnight," she told her potential customer, thinking it an easy out from the family invasion. "When is your son's birthday?"

"Next Monday. It coincides with his day off work."

Monday. Normally Samantha's day off, as well. But if she didn't accept this booking, what would she be doing? Trailing Helena all over who knew where—her mother had already asked where the nearest airport was in case she felt the need to call in the family jet—in search of the perfect home accessories. *No way.*

"We could start out Sunday afternoon," Samantha offered, "and return Monday afternoon. That wouldn't interfere with my other scheduled outings." And it would give her twenty-four hours away from Makeover Mother.

"Wonderful! Rory will be so excited."

"Rory?"

"Oh, I assumed you'd make the connection. But McQuire's a common name in that area."

"You're…?"

"Noelle McQuire. Rory's mother. He does work for you, doesn't he?"

"Y-yes." Samantha had been surprised and delighted he'd shown up at the farm this morning. On the job again. "He's a wonderful worker. A wonderful boy, really."

"Thank you." There was pride in Noelle McQuire's voice. "So, are they set for a Sunday overnight?"

"They?" The obvious began to dawn on Samantha.

"Rory and Garrett. His father. My ex. I'm assuming you know the sheriff."

"Of course." Did a shared kiss mean she knew the man? "And…yes, I guess we're set for the trek."

"Garrett will take care of the payment. Speaking of which, do you offer an employee discount?"

"I'm sure we can work something out." She wasn't worried about the money. Here she'd seen a way to avoid her mother's shopping binge, and now she found herself with a promised twenty-four-hours-worth of Garrett McQuire. Ah, yes, out of the frying pan into temptation's arms.

"Darling?" Her mother's voice startled her. "Do you want to see what I chose?"

Samantha stared at the phone in her hand, the line dead, and wondered how she'd gotten to this point. Had she at least signed off civilly? Sanely? "Wh-what did you choose?" she asked, pocketing the phone and turning to Helena.

"I think you saw the bench, but look at this fabulous pottery and these quilts…"

As her mother chattered on, Samantha wondered if they might not be buying back the items Red had sold.

"…now let's go get something cold to drink. How about the diner over there. Surely they make a decent sweet tea."

"They do," Samantha replied, glad to have a task that made some sense.

Several people walked by, openly interested in the limo and the uniformed chauffeur. One man—

Ziggy Newsome, Samantha seemed to remember—even stopped to ask how many miles per gallon the car got. Samantha hustled her mother away and across the street toward Rachel's Diner, only to see Garrett step out of the sheriff's headquarters and onto the sidewalk. Maybe he wouldn't notice—oh, God, he was heading right toward them.

"Afternoon." He actually tipped his Stetson, and, because his sunglasses were sticking out of his breast pocket, she could see his eyes. Piercing blue, fringed with incredibly thick, very dark lashes—and loaded with question. He looked from her to her mother.

"M-mother, this is Sheriff Garrett McQuire. His son, Rory, works for me. Sheriff, this is my mother, Helena Lawrence."

He cocked his head just slightly as he took in the last name, but recovered easily and shook her mother's hand. "Pleased to meet you."

"And I, you. Your town is charming. I can see why Ash…Samantha chose it for her…personal hiatus."

Garrett looked as if he didn't know what Helena was talking about. "Ms. Lawrence, I need to have a word with your daughter."

Helena eyed him carefully, then turned to Samantha. "I'll just go in and get us seated."

When her mother was inside the diner, Samantha

took the initiative. "This chat wouldn't be about Rory's birthday present, would it?"

"Yes. I was going to give you a heads-up. Did Rory talk to you about it this morning?"

"We didn't have a chance to speak. I saw him arrive as my group and I were heading out on the trail. Actually, Rory's mother called to make the arrangements."

"Noelle?"

"Yes. Seems because she won't be able to make Rory's birthday, she wanted to engineer something special."

He sighed. "My ex always goes for the deluxe package. But I don't understand how you could upgrade a hike. Rory's too young for champagne and he doesn't like caviar."

"Try an overnight." Samantha wanted to be blunt to catch his reaction. To see if he'd had any part in the plan. To see if he saw the kiss they'd shared as, maybe, the start of something.

"Are you nuts?" Apparently, he didn't.

From the corner of her eye, she saw her mother inside the diner, sitting at a window table, watching them.

"You didn't know about this?" A teeny, tiny part of Samantha was disappointed he hadn't plotted to engineer more time with her.

Garrett couldn't believe what he was hearing. Rory had asked for a *day,* not a whole night. Not that the idea of Samantha, a sleeping bag and a canopy of stars wasn't tempting. It was. But, right now, she didn't look tempted, and her mother, who was shooting him what he could only describe as the socialite's hairy eyeball, didn't seem open to letting her daughter share a sleeping bag—anytime, anywhere—with "the help."

What was going on here?

"Did you know about the overnight?" Samantha was asking him.

"No. Rory asked for a llama trek for his birthday. And for me to take the day off. I left it to him and his mother to make the arrangements." He paused. "Would it have made a difference, though, if I had been in on the planning?"

With her mother looking over her shoulder, Samantha seemed less self-possessed. Jumpier. "I guess that's neither here nor there, now," she said. "It's Rory who counts, right? By the way, I'm glad you decided he could come back to work."

Suddenly Garrett didn't want her to get the wrong idea. "Mack came to see me. He made a strong case for Rory's returning." He didn't want her to think he was a pushover. "Last night had nothing to do with my decision."

"Of course not. You were just—" she glanced over her shoulder at her mother "—distracting me from a sticky situation. I called my sponsor, by the way."

"Good…good. I'm glad we got over that hump."

"Me, too."

"So when did Noelle and you schedule this trek for?"

"I thought we'd take off Sunday afternoon, go along the ridge to the top of Russert's Mountain, camp by the lake, then come back down the next day."

Suddenly he didn't want the conversation to end. "Do you know much about overnight camping?"

She smiled, and he could see some of the old Samantha—or was it the new Samantha? "Let's just say I know a lot about llamas. But this will be a good test run to see if I want to expand my offerings down the road. Business offerings."

"Of course."

Rather imperiously, Helena Lawrence rapped on the window.

"I'd better get inside," Samantha said.

"I'll see you Sunday." Now why did he wish it was sooner?

At that moment Francis Beecham stuck his head around the diner door. "Sheriff! Can you come in and settle an argument?" Francis, Douglas Atwell and Owen Kent were Applegate's "official" retired coots.

During daylight hours they could be found either on one of the benches in front of the county courthouse, on stools at the diner or at a table at the barbecue shack. Their disagreements—which Garrett was often called in to settle—were loud and usually foolish. Noelle had always said these were the kind of people who encouraged hayseed sitcoms. Garrett didn't relish settling this particular spat in front of either Samantha or the Queen Mum.

But he held the diner door open for Samantha to enter.

"About the road bowling tournament," Francis said loudly as he drew Garrett to the counter.

Oh, no—

With a certain degree of trepidation, Samantha slid into the booth opposite her mother. There were two, tall and moist glasses of iced tea already on the table, and a little plate of Rachel's homemade macaroons.

"Whatever are they talking about?" Helena asked, eyeing the men at the counter.

"Nothing much. An upcoming tournament."

"One that involves cannonballs?" Her mother's eyes grew wide, incredulous. "Really, this town is too, too colorful."

"How's your tea?"

"Very good. Very cooling. Your sheriff should order some."

"Why?" Without thinking Samantha spoke the one word that could come back to bite her.

Helena leveled her catlike green gaze at her. "I do believe he has—what's that vulgar expression?—the hots for you."

"Mother!"

Everyone in the diner turned toward them. Helena countered their looks with a one-eyebrow-raised regal stare until they resumed their own conversations. And then she smiled at Samantha.

"Darling, of course the man would be attracted to you. And I must admit there's a raw sensuality about him—" Samantha nearly choked on an ice cube "—but if you put him side-by-side with Justin—"

"Justin is history."

"So you tell me. But I still can't help but think you two would have made the perfect match."

"No, Mother. Justin was looking for a merger. Not a marriage."

"Well, then forget Justin, but you can't sit here and tell me…" her mother lowered her voice considerably "…that the sheriff is an appropriate substitute."

Samantha lowered her voice even further. "Sheriff McQuire is the father of the boy who works for me. Period."

"His look said he'd like to be more."

"Okay." This was the stupidest discussion. "*If* the

man in question were interested, what should stop me from seeing if I might be interested?"

"I thought that was obvious," her mother said in exasperation, her voice rising with each word. "Applegate is just a diversion. You're not staying."

Everyone—including Garrett—swivelled to look at them again, yet this time Helena's imperious stare wasn't as effective in turning them back to their own business.

CHAPTER NINE

SUNDAY AFTERNOON GARRETT MADE a quick stop at headquarters before starting for Whistling Meadows, where Rory and Samantha were waiting for him. A couple of the deputies feigned shock at his civilian clothes. Said they hoped the department wouldn't self-destruct without him in the next twenty-four hours. Very funny.

Earlier that morning, Rory had been very specific about the personal items Garrett should put in a backpack that one of the llamas would be carrying. With great enthusiasm he'd explained llamas could carry fifty to sixty pounds of gear, and since they'd be transporting the camping equipment and the food, Samantha and he had had to allow for the weight of three personal packs. They were going to be taking Percy, Humvee and Mr. Jinx. And would Garrett, please, please, hurry. He'd then taken off on his bicycle to get to the farm first. Left alone, Garrett had packed, debating whether to bring along his service revolver. In the end, he made sure the safety was on and placed it in the backpack's outermost zipped pocket. He might be out of uniform, but he was the sheriff, and he was never off duty.

When he pulled into the Whistling Meadows barnyard, Rory was checking the packs on three llamas tethered to the inner-pasture fence while Samantha talked to Red. Seemed he was going to babysit the three remaining llamas. The old farmer still had some surprises up his sleeve.

"Hey," Garrett said, approaching his son but giving the hairy beasts a wide berth. For some reason they reminded him of variations on Big Bird. Tall, slightly goofy, with big soulful eyes. "Need any help?"

"No, thanks." With a great deal of concentration, Rory finished tightening a cinch, then turned to give Garrett the once-over. Apparently, his baseball cap, T-shirt, jeans and broken-in hiking boots passed muster. "Did you put on sunscreen and bug repellant?"

"Yeah, Ma." Garrett ruffled his son's hair. "I'm all greased up." Rory ducked out from under Garrett's hand but threw a playful punch at his upper arm.

Garrett held out his backpack. "So where do I put this?"

"On the llama you'll be leading?"

"Nobody said anything about being in charge of one of these things."

"That's part of the experience," Samantha said, approaching. She was dressed in hiking boots, voluminous khaki cargo pants and a plain white, figure-hugging T-shirt Garrett tried not to stare at. She'd lost all of her urban designer edge and recovered the equanimity she'd been missing when her mother was around. "Being in the company of llamas will lower your blood pressure, I guarantee it," she added.

Before he could think of a snappy comeback, he felt a shadow fall across his back, and in an instant his cap was lifted from his head. He turned to see a brown llama splashed with white triumphantly holding the cap visor in its mouth. The animal's head was just about even with Garrett's.

Rory chuckled. "Meet Percy. He's called a paint and he'll be your guide for this trek."

"I had to draw the class clown."

"Actually, we gave him to you because he has a dominant personality." Innocently, Samantha reached into one of the pockets of her cargo pants and retrieved a small handful of grain. Percy was happy to swap the cap for the treat. "Here," she said, pulling Garrett beyond the tether's reach. "You should be carrying some feed, too. It's a great motivator."

So maybe he should be munching some.

She slipped what looked like an Indian medicine pouch on a braided string over his head. "The campers at Rockbrook made these llama treat bags for us as a thank-you."

Oh, great. Next they'd expect him to wear a fanny pack.

Samantha shot him a bold look. "I'd let you carry the grain in your pocket, but your jeans are...quite snug." She smiled. "Better the pouch."

Was she going to give him shots the entire trip?

"Okay, Dad—" Rory cut in, taking the backpack out of Garrett's hands and expertly attaching it along-side the rest of the load on the paint "—you met Percy. And your stuff's right here where you can reach it. I'm going to be leading the black and tan. Humvee. And Samantha will be first on the trail with Mr. Jinx, the Appaloosa." He untied Percy and handed over the rope.

Garrett eyed Percy, who seemed to be smiling. "No tricks," he warned the animal.

"No tricks is right," Samantha repeated. "If Percy bolts, we lose the tents."

For the first time, Garrett really noted the camping equipment secured to the llama. It was ultra-light-weight, pop-up stuff. High-tech, and brand-new. "Did you just buy this?" he asked.

"Yes." Samantha led Mr. Jinx away from the fence toward the trailhead. "Mother was a tad disappointed to put aside buying stuff for the house to cruise the aisles of Wal-Mart, but, in her mind, shopping is shopping. It's all about the swipe of the plastic. I could even say, to her credit, she adapted."

Garrett ignored the pun. "So you're going to expand to overnight treks?"

"I don't know." She waved to Red, who was seated in a rocker on his porch. "Maybe."

It must be nice, Garrett thought with an involuntary tightening of his jaw, to go out on a moment's notice, without a thought to budget, and purchase top-of-the-line anything. Noelle's M.O. came to mind. She'd made the ability to do just that one of her goals. People like Noelle didn't often stick around Applegate. What had Helena Lawrence said—very clearly—to Samantha in the diner Thursday? *"Applegate is just a diversion. You're not staying."*

Garrett suddenly became disconcerted by the possibility that Samantha might be one rich—one spoiled rich?—woman, who was only temporarily playing at the simple life.

"Dad?" Rory's voice cut into his thoughts. "You ready? Just start walking behind Samantha. Percy will follow."

Actually, Percy led Garrett, alpha beast that he was.

Rory came up alongside, leading Humvee. "Do you notice how quiet they are? Not like horses. That's because they have pads on their feet, not hooves, so they don't have a negative impact on the environment. Cool, huh?"

He had to admit it was. "What are the bells on their halters for?" He liked having a conversation with his son, even if the topic was an unfamiliar one.

"To let animals on the trail know we're entering their territory."

The area was rich with deer, mountain lions, wolves and bears. "More to the point, how do we know if animals on the trail are invading our space?"

"Oh, the llamas will let us know. Percy especially. It's the llama scream." Rory shuddered. "I heard it once when a fox crossed their pasture. These guys are like burglar alarms. Did you know they're sometimes used to guard sheep and goats?"

"How'd you get so smart, kid?" Proud of his son, Garrett told himself to breathe. To forget about Samantha—her life was her life, and his was his—and concentrate on Rory. This outing was, after all, his son's birthday wish. "Chip off the old smart block, huh?"

But he couldn't get Samantha out of his thoughts. She was right in his line of sight, up ahead on the trail that started in the outer pasture—the one they'd crossed in their escape from Tanner—and wound up into the forest. Sixty acres made for one beautiful personal playground.

Although Red had never let on how much his property had fetched, Garrett knew the going rate around here. Bushels.

He had to stop focusing on Samantha and her situation. "So," he said to Rory, "you have any idea what she's going to feed us?"

"Not a clue. But there's a lot of it. Humvee has the coolers. If we don't like what she packed, we can always fish."

Garrett noted the large food containers as well as three brand-new fishing rods. Samantha had spared no expense. The local economy had received a shot in the arm. So what was Mr. Jinx up ahead carrying—a new bass boat?

He tried not to take a jaundiced view, but he'd feel a whole lot better about Samantha if he knew this llama business was of her own making, the fruits of her planning, hard work and a savings account, and not some offhand hobby gifted from Mommy and Daddy.

Samantha could feel Garrett watching her, but today it didn't bother her. The fresh, open air, the beautiful mountains, the presence of animals that could only be described as Zen masters diffused the man's brooding intensity. Nothing could darken her mood on the trail. On land that made her feel real. Not the remodeling of the farmhouse. Not the fact that she'd almost fallen off the wagon this week. Not even the fact that Garrett didn't seem to be enjoying this hike the way she and Rory had hoped.

Stiff and preoccupied didn't begin to describe him.

They passed through the gate that separated the outer pasture from the forest and were walking along a spongy carpet of sweet-smelling pine needles. Cardinals—brilliant flashes of red—swooped overhead in the pattern of light and shadow created by the rustling tree branches.

"Hey, what's he doing?" Behind her Garrett's voice cut across the quiet. "Is this going to make him sick? Believe me, I don't have llama rental insurance and I don't make enough money to replace him."

She turned to see Percy had stopped and was grazing on the fallen needles. "He's okay." She led Mr. Jinx around to come abreast of the others. "Those and dried leaves are like potato chips to the boys."

Garrett looked dubious. "Then how come your two aren't chowing down?"

"I think Percy's testing you a little. Do you want to swap leads? Mr. Jinx is very biddable."

Garrett eyed her as if this were some kind of challenge. "We're fine."

"It's not like we're punching a clock, Dad," Rory said. "If we don't make it to the lake by nightfall, we pitch the tents wherever."

When Mr. Jinx sniffed the ground next to Percy,

Percy raised his head and spit a mouthful of needles at the younger llama. Laughing, Samantha pulled Mr. Jinx away from Percy's grazing.

"What was that all about?" Garrett asked.

"Territoriality." She looked right at Garrett and wondered if a part of his prickliness was because he saw her as usurping some of his son's attention this summer.

"The infamous llama spit?"

"No," Rory replied, smiling. "That was just stage one. A warning. If Mr. Jinx ignored it, Percy would give him the saliva treatment."

"Gross."

"Gross, but not the grossest. If Mr. Jinx were stupid enough to disregard stage two, Percy would throw the big green spit. The contents of his stomach."

"I don't think I need to be hearing this."

"Wait, there's more!" Rory was really getting into this. It was good to see he was twelve going on thirteen and not a little man, worrying about the adults around him. "Llamas can spit with dead aim ten to fifteen feet!"

"Have you been teaching him this?" Garrett asked, looking at Samantha. She was pleased to see he was smiling. Even big boys were suckers for the yucky stuff.

"No, sir. Your son is a keen observer." And Rory

had let her know that he'd been watching his dad, too. And worrying that he worked too hard and played too little.

"He's not going to turn on me, is he?"

"Not likely. Here." She dug in another one of her pockets for some raisins. "These are extra-special treats. Offer Percy a few of these and he'll follow you anywhere." She dropped several in Garrett's hand, then watched his face as Percy delicately picked up one at a time. She knew the sensation. Soft and whiskery. And sensual.

A look of awe suffused Garrett's rugged features. "I'd say this guy has opposable lips."

Behind Garrett's back, Rory sent her a thumbs-up.

"Now you two lead the way," she suggested. "That will make Percy very happy."

As first Garrett, then Rory, headed up the trail, the llamas' halter bells tinkling softly, she followed, hopeful the starched and pressed sheriff had been dropped by the wayside. She knew what it meant to be tied up in one's job to the exclusion of relationships, of other options, of one's own happiness. For her, rehab had been more than a solution to a drinking problem. It had been the start of finding out who she really was. Where her true priorities lay.

She stopped to absorb her surroundings. The afternoon was gorgeous with blue skies, brilliant sun and puffy clouds. In the distance she could see receding purplish silhouettes of the Blue Ridge Mountains. The farther they climbed, the cooler the air became. From her personal pack she pulled a sweatshirt. Drawing it over her head, she took a moment to inhale the fresh, line-dried scent of it. She needed to point out these tiny perks of country living to her mother, who still referred to Samantha's choice as "temporarily roughing it."

Suddenly, from up ahead, a llama's shrill alarm call rang out, then seconds later gunfire. Her llamas! Rory! Garrett! Dear God, what was going on?

Her heart thumping wildly against her ribs, she pulled Mr. Jinx in the direction of the shots. As she rounded a stone outcropping on the trail she saw Rory, Humvee's lead firmly in hand, chasing Percy, who was loose and running farther up the trail.

Garrett was standing on the path, a revolver in his hand.

Quickly looping Mr. Jinx's lead to a low-lying branch, Samantha ran to confront Garrett. "What—"

It was then she saw the timber rattlesnake. Or pieces of it. Before Garrett had dispatched it, it had been maybe five feet long and had probably been sunning on the trailside ledge that was hip high. Its beautiful yellow body with brown crossbands was now scattered in a bloody mess on the granite rocks.

She couldn't contain her fury. "What the hell do you think you're doing?"

"Percy recognized the danger before I did," Garrett replied, scowling at her onslaught. "The rattler was poised to strike."

Anger rendered her speechless. She glared at him. In the early months of settling in, she'd taken extension courses on land management. She was drawn to the environmentalists, the conservationists who recognized each animal's necessary niche in nature and rejected the old school of simply killing what you considered a varmint. She'd vowed not on her property. No way.

Her hands shook so badly, she had to jam them in her pockets. "You...brought...*a gun* on this outing?" She could barely keep herself from stuttering.

"My service revolver. And the question might be why you're not armed." Garrett looked her right in the eye. Samantha might have a soft heart and good intentions, but she needed a hard lesson in protecting herself and her interests. "You could have lost your llama."

"Not if you'd moved him out of harm's way. Instead of playing some loose-cannon cowboy."

Now that hurt. "You can't predict a rattler. And your property's not going to suffer because you're now one short. My first priority is to protect."

"Where did you have that…that *thing?*" She pointed with disgust at his revolver.

"In my backpack."

"On my llama!"

"I assure you the safety was on. And, yeah, I have all the necessary papers allowing me to carry a concealed weapon."

"You weren't carrying it! Percy was!"

As they faced off, Rory reappeared, leading both Humvee and Percy. "Dad, how could you bring your revolver?" he cried, tying the two llamas next to Mr. Jinx, then coming to stand solidly next to Samantha. He fairly shook with indignation, and Garrett couldn't understand either his outrage or hers.

"Y'all seem to forget I'm the sheriff. I carry a weapon. Son, you've grown up with guns in the house, and we've gone over and over the safety issues. The responsibility issues."

"But I asked you to take a day off."

Garrett still didn't understand.

"For my birthday I didn't want you to be the sheriff. I just wanted you to be my dad."

Garrett's mouth went dry as both Samantha and Rory glared at him. Despite all the maturity his son had exhibited earlier in the day, he was still a kid. With a kid's needs.

"Rory, I'm your dad first and foremost." How

could he explain he would take on more than a rattler, if necessary? He was prepared to take on the world. For his only child. "I'm not sorry I killed the snake. I used my best judgment there. I'm sorry if I made you feel you weren't getting all of me today. You are."

Rory scuffed the ground with the toe of his boot. "Okay." He looked sideways at Samantha. "Are you okay?"

Narrowing her eyes at Garrett, she didn't appear quite as willing to forgive. "What are you planning to do with the gun for the rest of the trek?"

"I sure can't leave it by the wayside. Look—" he carefully demonstrated engaging the safety "—it'll be all right in the backpack."

She didn't budge.

"I did bring a shoulder holster if—"

"No! I don't want to see it."

"It'll be okay on Percy," Rory assured her. "Dad knows what he's doing."

He appreciated Rory's vote of confidence, but the way Samantha looked at him now—as if she didn't trust him—made Garrett aware he'd radically altered the dynamics of this trip.

The rest of the trek up Russert's Mountain to the lake was unnaturally silent. Garrett couldn't believe he actually welcomed Percy's company.

CHAPTER TEN

THE AFTERNOON SHADOWS HAD grown very long as the group approached the lake. Samantha had been stunned into silence by Garrett's macho display back on the trail. Sure, he was the sheriff—and obviously, like her father, his job totally defined who he was— but couldn't he, at least, have left his service revolver behind on his son's birthday? When she got back to the farmhouse, she was going to have to rewrite her flyers to include some trek prohibitions.

"Oh, no!" Up ahead Rory and Humvee had entered the clearing near the lake where they were supposed to camp. "Who would have done this?"

She heard a sharp explosive *"Damn"* from Garrett.

When she came alongside them, she saw the awful mess. Someone had used the area as party central. A huge fire pit, now blackened, had been dug near the lake. The surrounding area was littered with empty beer cans and crumpled fast-food wrappers. An aluminum chair, an old tire and a large cooler could be seen just under the surface of the lake several yards out from the shore. Feeling sick, Samantha covered her mouth with one hand as she turned to survey the surrounding rock outcroppings spray-painted with expletives.

She felt violated.

Rory and Garrett came to stand on either side of her. "Don't worry," Rory said. "We can clean this up." He took all three llamas' leads. "I'm gonna find a place to tether these guys where they can't munch on anything lethal."

As he led the boys a little way back down the trail, Garrett said, "Before we disturb anything, you need to let me look around the area. To see if I can find anything that might tell us who did this. Although I'd lay odds it was the Harris boys and their friends." He indicated a cluster of rocks near the water's edge. "Have a seat. I won't be long."

"I want to start cleaning up." Maybe then the gnawing sensation in the pit of her stomach would stop.

"We'll all pitch in," Garrett assured her. When Rory came back, he added, "I'm going to have a look around. Stay with Samantha."

"Sure." Rory sat on a rock next to her. "It's gonna be okay. We're gonna help you."

"But the paint…" With dismay she stared at the now defaced wall of rocks.

"Red and I will take care of that tomorrow. The maintenance staff in my school back in Charlotte have a special goop they use to cover graffiti. If we can't get it from the hardware store here in town, my mom will find out what it is and have it sent. Don't worry."

Samantha couldn't help smiling at this kid's simple optimism, his can-do attitude, his chivalry. "Thank you," she tried to say, but found herself choking on tears.

"Aw-w-w, don't cry." Clumsily, he patted her back. "I hate it when girls cry."

"This is a terrible birthday present."

"Yeah. I demand a refund." He grinned. "Just kidding."

Garrett returned, scowling. "Where are the No Trespassing signs Red had posted?"

"I—I took them down. They seemed so confrontational."

"They served a purpose." It looked as if he might deliver a lecture, then thought better of it. He held out his hand to her. "Come on. Let's take care of this mess. Did you bring any trash bags?"

"Yes." When she took his hand he pulled her to her feet. They stood looking at one another, and she could see not simply a sheriff, but a person who felt her pain over the desecration of this place.

"Mack and I used to camp out when we were kids," he said. "We weren't big on observing boundaries, but we loved the land. These kids feel nothing. I don't know how you combat that."

Just when she was determined not to forgive him for the snake incident, he had to show a sensitive side.

The tethered llamas were contentedly munching low-hanging leaves when she retrieved the box of trash bags from Mr. Jinx's pack.

"I'm assuming you'll need to tend to these guys, so Rory and I'll start the cleanup."

Startled that Garrett had followed her, she turned around quickly to find him standing very close.

"Are you okay?" he asked.

"I will be. It was a shock, seeing such a pretty place defiled."

"I'm just glad you weren't alone." He frowned, yet his eyes showed concern. "Aren't alone."

"Me, too." As she handed him the trash bags, she realized what a breakthrough admission that was. In constructing the Singapore Ashley, she'd handled issues far more difficult than graffiti and garbage. Of course, she'd relied on experts for the building process, but the problems, the glitches, the setbacks she'd handled herself. Without consulting her father. Her ability to take the reins solo was something she had to prove to herself. It was her badge of honor. And, ultimately, her undoing.

She watched Garrett walk away. So strong himself, did he see her as weak? Or was he able to recognize in her, as she had in Mack, a fellow human being whose pain deserved respect?

Turning to unload the llamas, Samantha instantly felt an easing of her agitation. Their patience, their gentle humming, their looks that seemed to say, "You humans make life so complicated," allowed her to find her center.

The physical exertion helped, too. Unloading tents and coolers and personal backpacks, she placed them far enough up the trail that the llamas couldn't reach them, yet not so close to the lake area as to be in Garrett and Rory's way.

Although the treetops along the ridge were gilded with sunlight, an early twilight had descended here in the lake basin. Once the llamas were free of their loads, they assumed a *kush* position. Chewing their cuds, they settled in for a well-deserved rest.

Samantha retrieved a pair of work gloves from her backpack before returning to the campsite, where she found Garrett and Rory hip deep in the lake, wrestling with a waterlogged tire. Having made quite a pile of trash just outside the clearing, they were soaked and thoroughly mucked up and looked as if they were having the time of their lives.

"We thought we'd get the heavy stuff first," Garrett called out when he saw Samantha. He couldn't keep the pride and pleasure from his voice. Rory was handling this whole situation like a man. And he was discovering how good it felt to work alongside his son. As equals.

"Some of that junk is a health hazard," he remarked as Samantha shook out a garbage bag with a determined set to her shoulders. "I'm glad to see you have gloves."

"All the better to strangle whoever did this," she replied with a ferocity that surprised him. When they'd first come upon the scene, he'd been afraid she was going to fall apart.

He hated to admit it, but as soon as Samantha joined them, his focus became fragmented. He found himself watching her as she set about the task at hand with an energy equal to either his or Rory's—but with a certain vulnerability mixed with her competence. This trashing of a special place on her property had rattled her, highlighting that she wasn't from here. Didn't understand that these things—unpleasant as they were—happened in an area where the kids had limited opportunities both in the job market and in recreation. If Red still owned the property, the No Trespassing signs would be strictly enforced. The old man would shoot up anyone who disregarded them, knowing the local law was on his side.

"I think that does it for the lake," Rory said, startling Garrett out of his thoughts.

"Good job, son." He turned to Samantha. "Since we're already dirty, we can take over the garbage pickup around the fire pit and you can begin to set up camp. We'll clear a place for the tents first."

Suddenly, Samantha looked very unsure of herself.

"What's wrong?"

"N-nothing." Without another word she turned back down the trail to where the llamas were tied and the equipment stacked.

As Garrett picked up the trash and Rory swept the ground smooth with an evergreen branch, Samantha schlepped the folded tents, the coolers, the personal backpacks and what seemed like a ton of miscellaneous equipment. And then she hesitated.

"I'm going to look for firewood," Rory said. "And then I'm having a swim to cool off."

"Need help?" Garrett asked Samantha.

She didn't answer.

"What's wrong?"

She was staring at the tents, which, in their present state lying unassembled on the ground, looked like three large strips of freeze-dried seaweed. There was a little-girl-lost expression on her face.

He washed his hands in the lake before coming to stand next to her. "Have you ever been camping before?"

The in-control woman quickly snapped to attention. "Of course I have."

"Where?"

"In Kenya. On safari."

Now there was a different ballgame. "Did you put up your own tents?" He could see the answer coming.

"No. We had…attendants." She sighed. "But how hard can it be? These were advertised as extremely easy trail models."

He knelt down to examine them. He'd give her credit for buying top-of-the-line. Nothing like the primitive lean-tos Mack and he had constructed as kids—when they'd even bothered to put shelter over their heads. He found the appropriate tab on the first tent and pulled. The thing popped up like a toadstool after a spring rain.

"Wow, that makes me feel foolish!" she exclaimed.

He wanted to ask her if she was the kind of person who had to have a handle on everything in every situation. If this drive for perfection had driven her to drink. Instead, he busied himself locating the tab on the second tent. "Okay, your turn."

She pulled the tab, and, as the second tent sprang

up, she laughed. "This is as much fun as popping bubble wrap."

"Then the third one's yours." He didn't quite share her enthusiasm for either pastime, but he was mesmerized by Samantha herself. By how she could be strong and vulnerable, sad and happy, exotic and down-to-earth all at the same time.

She was someone who, if he'd met her under different circumstances, would definitely spark an interest. Who was he kidding? She already had. Problem was, he'd bet his last dollar she'd be gone before the fall leaves turned color. Gone with nothing remaining but a For Sale sign stuck by Whistling Meadows' roadside.

Scowling, he made himself busy securing the tents a safe distance from the fire pit.

"Hey, those are really cool tents." Rory came back with an armload of firewood. "Looks like I'm just in time. It's getting dark."

"If you start the fire," Samantha said, taking foil-wrapped packages out of the cooler, "I'll start supper."

"What are we having?"

"Red's Surprise. At least, that's what he calls it. Spicy chicken and veggies. I just followed his directions."

Placing sleeping bags and backpacks in each tent, Garrett listened to the easy conversation between his

son and this woman who'd arrived in town to capti-
vate just about everyone. He thought about Noelle,
who had been raised here, and how she'd never
seemed to fit in. How when they'd married and had
Rory she'd always refused to go on family camping
trips. Her idea of roughing it was anything less than
a suite at one of the best hotels. Then he thought
about how good it felt to be celebrating his son's
birthday on a llama trek, of all things, and tried not
to fall under Samantha's spell.

"Hey." She spoke so softly he was startled to find
her standing right next to him. "You forgot the air
mattresses."

"This must be the Ritz version of camping out."

He thought he saw her flinch. "Let's just say this
is a prototype trek. I'm counting on your feedback.
If I choose to offer overnights, I want them to be en-
joyable. Comfortable."

Ah, yes. There it was. He'd forgotten that to her
this was business. He suspected the whole llama operation was just an experiment. Maybe it would fly,
maybe not. With her parents' money behind her, no
big deal. He'd intended to join Rory in that swim
after they'd finished setting up. Call his sudden realization an advanced splash of cold water.

Samantha wondered at Garrett's cool stare. "You
don't want an air mattress?"

"Sure, you can put one under my sleeping bag. If it goes with the package deal, why not?" He looked toward Rory, who was tethering the three llamas closer to the campsite. "You ready for that swim?" he asked his son.

"You bet."

"Last one in's a rotten egg!"

Before Samantha could say she'd forgotten to bring towels, man and boy kicked off their hiking boots, then raced down the embankment in the growing darkness to throw themselves—fully clothed—into the water, where their shouts echoed off the mountains.

The primitive nature of their play captivated her. An only child, she'd always been exhorted to behave "like a lady." When she'd been able to escape to her father's stables, she'd done so with the proper riding habit, the proper equipment, the proper horse. Proper. Even the family's hotel empire was aimed at a clientele who fundamentally appreciated *proper* even as they craved luxurious. She couldn't imagine one of the guests at the Singapore Ashley romping in a frigid mountain lake. Funny, but now she found it hard to picture herself even standing in the lobby of any one of her father's properties.

As she finished inflating the air mattresses and putting one in each of the tents, she resisted the urge to throw a little granola on the top of each sleeping bag. Gourmet chocolate, who needed it?

Turning toward the fire to check on supper, she saw a most amazing sight. Garrett had emerged from the lake. As he walked up the embankment, he was stripping off his T-shirt, revealing a rock-hard chest, muscles rippling in the firelight. Without an ounce of self-consciousness, he flung the wet shirt over a low-lying tree branch, then un-buttoned his jeans.

When she gasped, he stopped, and Rory, shaking like a dog, plowed into the back of him.

"I—I didn't bring towels," she said.

"Don't need 'em," he replied with a slow quirk on one side of his mouth. "We each brought a change of clothes. These'll be dry enough in the morning."

Rory checked each tent for his backpack. When he found it, he started to strip. "Samantha, turn away. Puleeze."

She didn't know where to look. If she turned away from Rory, she could see Garrett, who hadn't moved and who was regarding her with a sexy twinkle of amusement. "I take it you didn't have brothers."

"No." Grabbing a pair of tongs, she knelt by the fire to flip the foil packets she'd tucked in the coals. The parcels sizzled and emitted a wonderful aroma of cooking meat and vegetables. Red had assured her it was the hungry man special. Quick and easy. "Supper's almost ready."

Behind her the sounds of rustling could only mean Garrett, too, was changing into dry clothes. Supper she could control. Her imagination she could not.

A bat swooped overhead as the stars began to appear in the night sky. The fire crackled, sending sparks into the air. And despite the unsettling attraction she felt for one sheriff out of uniform, Samantha felt a peace descend on her. Out here on Russert's Mountain—her land—she didn't have to be anyone other than Samantha Weston. A woman who owned llamas and made a decent camp meal. If she didn't yet know exactly who she was, this was a good start.

"Smells good." Garrett appeared by her side.

She stood, then looked him in the eye. Sort of resisting temptation by confronting it. "You've got to stop sneaking up on me."

"I might be accused of doing many things," he replied with a wry smile, "but sneaking isn't one of them." He took the tongs from her hands. "I'll watch supper if you want to take a dip."

"I—I wasn't planning on it." Now why did her pulse pick up? "I'm chief cook and bottle washer here. You're the guests."

"I think we're beyond that. Unless—" he cast a glance over his shoulder at the stacks of trash bags just beyond the perimeter of the campsite "—litter patrol was part of the recreation program."

"It wasn't. And I thank you for your help."

"Does it make up for the rattlesnake?" There wasn't so much apology in his gaze as a real concern for her feelings on the subject.

Before she could answer, Rory rolled a big log up to the fire. "I'm starving."

"I see you brought your own chair," Samantha replied as she found the mess kits.

Garrett retrieved the food packets from the fire and placed them on a nearby rock. Expertly, he folded back the foil on one, then poured the contents into the mess kit Samantha held out. The spiced chicken, peppers, onions, tomatoes and corn on the cob made her mouth water, but she handed the first portion to Rory. The second she offered Garrett, but he said, "Go ahead, eat. I'll get this last one."

"I hope you brought stuff to make s'mores," Rory said around a mouthful as Samantha took a seat beside him on the log.

"You bet. How's the chow?"

"Excellent. Red can't say you're a lousy cook anymore."

"Did he really say I was a lousy cook?" She laughed. "Well, I was. But I'm not now." And that, in a nutshell, could be her life motto.

"Scoot down." His own supper in hand, Garrett strode over to the log.

Instead of sitting next to Rory, where there was room, he was standing at her end, which clearly had no room for anyone else. Before she could point out the obvious, Rory obligingly moved, and Samantha found herself sandwiched between the two guys. Rory gave her space, but Garrett didn't.

"I want to know if you're still angry with me over the rattlesnake," he said.

She'd let her anger go as soon as Garrett had understood how important it was to restore some sense of order to the campsite. Even if she hadn't forgiven him then, it would have been difficult to remain annoyed with him now while his thigh rested against hers. Call her a fool, but there was something basic and very appealing about his touch.

"No," she replied, "I'm not mad at you. Why do you ask?"

He turned to look directly at her. "Maybe because your good opinion of me matters."

That might have been the loveliest thing anyone had ever said to her. Paying customer or not, the man was clearly taking unfair advantage.

CHAPTER ELEVEN

AT THE CRACK OF DAWN, SAMANTHA crawled out of her sleeping bag to feed the llamas. When she opened the tent flap, she saw four figures standing absolutely still in the lake just offshore. As swallows darted overhead, Garrett fished. Surrounding him, the three llamas looked as if they might be offering advice.

She stood, stretched, then slowly, so as not to disturb the fascinating tableau, walked barefoot down to the water's edge. She noticed trout already caught and strung on a line in the shallows, just waiting for the breakfast frying pan.

Percy was the first to notice her. He waded over and snuffled her pocket for a treat. "I have something better," she whispered, stroking his neck. "A bowl of mash."

"Good morning," Garrett said quietly, turning to gift her with a smile.

Who knew *anyone* could look that gorgeous so early in the morning? Self-consciously, she swiped at the sleep-disheveled tendrils of hair that dangled near her face.

"I thought these guys might want off their tethers," he said. "I have to admit they're good company. Quieter than most people. A lot calmer than dogs."

Aw, he'd fallen prey to llama charm.

Rolling up her khakis, she waded out in the chill water to stand next to him, to prolong the moment before feeding the boys. Percy followed. "Where's Rory?"

"Asleep. You didn't happen to bring any birthday candles, did you?"

"I sure did. And a cake. For lunch on the way down."

"Could I use one of the candles?" he asked. "I want to stick it in Rory's breakfast trout. It's not every day a boy turns thirteen."

At that moment she fell for the sheriff.

Growing up, she'd always had elaborate, catered birthday celebrations that made her want to hide in order to catch her breath. She would have loved to have one or both parents all to herself for the day. And she would have traded all the fancy cakes for a trout with a candle in it for breakfast.

"You're a wonderful father," she said softly.

"Thanks." He seemed disconcerted by the compliment.

"I mean it. Rory's the proof."

He didn't answer but played with his fishing line. The llamas were statue-still. More swallows swooped over the surface of the water, catching insects. The sky was a brilliant blue, but here in this hollow, protected by tall evergreens, the sun's rays hadn't yet penetrated. The lake, with wisps of mist rising from its surface, was shrouded in an early morning opalescence. Samantha had the feeling she'd been transported to a fairyland.

"Don't move," Garrett said, quietly breaking the silence. "You have a dragonfly on the top of your head."

Despite his command, she bent to look at her reflection in the water, and, there on the top of her head, like a fantastic barrette, sat the large lace-winged insect. It seemed so unreal she couldn't help lifting her hand to feel it. Of course, it flew away. When she raised her head, Garrett was looking at her with a gaze so intense it made her shiver.

"Sometimes you just want to touch beauty," he said before slipping his free hand behind her neck and pulling her into a deep kiss.

Not even raising her arms, she leaned against him and let herself float on the kiss. Let the heat of his mouth and the coldness from the lake water meet somewhere in the very center of her, creating a tumultuous eddy that made her deliciously dizzy.

Neither of them pulled away. It was as if they

simply drifted apart. With half-closed eyes she stood looking at him looking at her. As if he wanted more. Much more. It had to be the magic of the place.

Percy chose that moment to put his head between them. He turned first to one and then the other as his big liquid-brown eyes seemed to say, "All this communing is fine, but what about that mash you promised me?"

Garrett chuckled. "First Ruggiero, now Percy. I'd like to see what might evolve if your chaperones weren't so conscientious."

Oh, she knew exactly what would evolve. But at this stage in her life, when she felt so emotionally tentative, she didn't think it wise to leave matters of the heart to natural selection.

She stepped away from him. "I'm going to feed the llamas. Are you preparing breakfast?"

"Yes. The menu features trout, trout and more trout."

"If you're interested, there are precooked potatoes in the cooler, for home fries."

"I'm interested."

Gathering up the boys' halter lines, she led them to shore, wondering if the sheriff's interest was confined to breakfast ingredients.

Suddenly, Garrett felt powerfully hungry. He reeled in his line, then quickly cleaned the fish he'd already caught. When he'd first gotten up, he'd rebuilt the fire. Although the flames had now died down, the coals were hot and cooking-ready. The skillets Samantha had provided were—of course—state-of-the-art. He rummaged in the cooler for the potatoes, and only when trout and home fries were sizzling in their pans and coffee was perking, did he allow himself the opportunity to watch Samantha with the llamas.

She was fast becoming his guilty pleasure.

Dressed in khaki and flannels like any ordinary hiker, she was far from ordinary. A strength lay under her delicacy. Mystery underscored her beauty. And in her kisses he detected both reserve and the potential for abandonment. But he could sense nothing that indicated the two of them had much chance of a relationship in the real world. That was why he wished the camping trip wouldn't end.

"Something smells good." Yawning and scratching, Rory crawled out of his tent.

"Happy birthday, son." Garrett lit a candle, then stuck it in one of the cooked trout. "Don't ask me to sing."

"Thanks, Dad." With a cockeyed grin, Rory accepted his breakfast and sleepily sat on the log. "This is the best birthday ever."

Samantha returned to place a small wrapped present on the log next to Rory. "Happy birthday.

This is just a little something. It can wait until you've eaten."

Handing Samantha a plate of food and a cup of coffee, Garrett couldn't help wondering what it would be like to face this woman every morning over breakfast.

"This is beyond delicious." Fork raised, she looked at him across the fire, her hazel eyes wide. "Are you always this handy in the kitchen?"

"Only if trout is involved."

"Is there more?" Rory held out his plate.

"Do you have a hollow leg?" Garrett divvied up the remainder of the fish and potatoes between his son and himself. His own first helping. But there were no complaints. The fact that his thirteen-year-old child still wanted to be with him, still appreciated what he had to offer was worth any hunger pangs he might experience farther down the trail.

He could feel Samantha watching this exchange. "I wish we didn't have to go back," she said, echoing his own thoughts.

But back they had to go. All three pitched in to break camp, leaving the area spotless except for the spray-painted graffiti on the rocks. Garrett made a silent promise to help Rory and Red with that cleanup. On the final leg of the homeward trek, no one spoke, but it was a contented silence. They even passed the granite outcropping where he'd dispatched the rattlesnake, without so much as a sideways glance from Samantha. Garrett noticed because he'd finagled the second spot in line, where eyes on the person ahead of you wasn't considered an offense.

How many times had he told himself he was reluctant to reenter the real world?

When the Whistling Meadows outer pasture came into sight, Rory moved alongside Garrett on the trail.

"Hey, what did Samantha give you back at the campsite?" he asked his son.

Rory pulled from his pocket an incredible Swiss Army knife that Garrett knew for sure would bust his budget.

"Cool, huh?" Rory said, smiling. "But you know what was almost as good a birthday present as the trek and this?"

"What?"

"That you shut your cell phone off."

"Hey, if you can go without your cell phone and your video games and your iTunes, I had to show I was just as strong."

"Bet Mom's ticked she couldn't get hold of us."

Oh, yeah. There would be messages from Noelle that would singe his ears.

Having stopped at the gate, Samantha was staring

in dismay at the farmhouse in the distance. "What's going on?" she exclaimed. Garrett and Rory hustled to catch up.

Far below, the barnyard was alive with activity. Samantha could see her parents' limo, as well as several service vans, plus a very large delivery truck. People were scurrying between the vehicles and the farmhouse. Which was now painted a color Helena would call "quaint cottage yellow."

"Oh, no! Mother, you haven't!" Samantha cried as she flung open the gate and charged into the outer pasture, Mr. Jinx in tow. "Rory, close the gate behind you!" she shouted over her shoulder as she made her way toward a scene out of *Trading Spaces*. Mr. Jinx's pack clanked and rattled as he trotted along beside her, ears up, anticipating excitement.

This wasn't excitement, this was a home invasion.

As she skirted the inner pasture, Mephisto, Ace and Fred dashed up to the fence to greet them and began an antelope-like *pronking* that would have made Samantha laugh had she not been so exasperated at what she knew awaited her.

Rounding the barn, she came face-to-face with Red, who reached out for Mr. Jinx's lead. "I tried to stop her," the old man said with as much agitation as she felt. "Not that you can't do what you want to the place. It's yours now and no business of mine.

But when she said this was to be a surprise, I got a bad feeling."

"You couldn't have stopped her, Red. But I can."

"I think it's too late, but I'll take care of Jinxy here. You go."

She didn't have to be told twice. As she crossed the yard, she had to watch out for painters, carpenters, electricians and people carrying furniture and floral arrangements. Floral arrangements? What did Helena think this was, a hotel opening?

Dashing up the porch steps, she noticed the space just in front of her house had been totally landscaped. She now had an instant emerald-green lawn where hard-packed dirt had been, and up against the porch foundation flower beds had appeared with a profusion of blooms. The newly painted porch was dotted with tastefully grouped wicker furniture that looked as if it might feel more at home on the veranda of a Newport summer cottage.

"No, no, no, you absolutely can't come in yet!" her mother exclaimed breathlessly, emerging from the house and barring Samantha's way. "We didn't expect you quite so soon. Mr. Harris was supposed to warn me when he saw you."

"What are you doing to my home?" Samantha asked as Cameron's booming voice came from inside, shouting out orders.

"Your father and I felt that if you insisted on continuing your recuperation here in Applegate, you should at least do it in some comfort."

"This isn't my recuperation," Samantha replied with a sinking heart. "This is my life."

"All the more reason your surroundings should suit it."

"What's going on?" Garrett's voice behind her was the best thing she could have heard. But when she turned to look at him, she saw disapproval on his face.

"Sheriff, maybe you can talk some sense into Samantha," Helena said. "Just one more hour, and we'll be ready. If she comes in now, she just won't receive the true effect. So would you be a dear and take her for a walk?"

"Ma'am, with all due respect, we just finished walking. I think Samantha deserves to go in her own house, take a long hot shower and put her feet up."

"But—"

Garrett reached behind Helena, opened the door, then held it for Samantha. She couldn't have been more grateful.

Stepping through the doorway, however, her gratitude and every other emotion with the exception of utter shock evaporated. The interior of her once simple farmhouse was unrecognizable.

Every surface had been repainted. Every light

fixture replaced. Where there had been lovely space, there was now very expensive furniture. And window treatments. And paintings. And those damned flower arrangements. It was the re-creation of a world in which her old self had lived. Everything was so tasteful it made her sick.

"How long have we been gone?" Garrett asked.

Growing more frustrated by the second, Samantha turned to her mother. "This wasn't some spur-of-the-moment idea, was it?"

"No. Your father and I had been considering the possibility on our ride here. We contacted our people and had them on standby."

"But the physical execution," Samantha said. "We haven't been gone twenty-four hours."

"Darling, you know nothing's impossible when money's no object."

Samantha felt Garrett stiffen. By the time Cameron came out of the kitchen to envelope her in his signature bear hug, the sheriff had disappeared.

GARRETT COULDN'T BREATHE. Standing outside on the too-cute stone walkway, he thought of the money that had gone into that "surprise." More money than was budgeted yearly for his entire department, he'd bet. Conspicuous consumption. He had no use for it.

Who exactly were these people?

He walked to the barn to retrieve his backpack, which held his revolver and his cell phone. Having unloaded the llama packs and sent Mr. Jinx, Humvee and Percy into the inner pasture to relax with the rest of the herd, Rory and Red were sorting the camp equipment.

"Rory," Garrett said. "I think Samantha's supposed to do that. We're the paying customers." That might be true, but he'd forgotten to discuss the fee with her, and she hadn't brought it up.

Red shot him a look. "The Duchess has her hands full, I'd say."

The Duchess. The nickname rang so true.

"Dad, I like doing this." Rory seemed to be in his element. So much so, Garrett wondered what Noelle—a duchess in her own right—would say if she saw their son now. Disheveled. Sweaty. And absolutely happy. "But I know you wanna get back to the department. I have my bike. You can go."

He did need to check in. Pick up his messages. Get out of here. "See you at home."

"See ya. And Dad? I had a great time."

"So did I." Too bad it had to end with a big dose of reality.

Heading for the cruiser, he took out his cell phone. Seventeen messages from Noelle alone. Rather than listen to them, he called her.

She picked up on the first ring. "I got the promotion!"

"Congratulations," he said warily. "When do you start?"

"Just as soon as I can put the Charlotte condo on the market. I've been house hunting around London this afternoon. Sticker shock does not begin to describe the experience, but it'll be so worth it. Rory can choose to attend one of the American corporation schools or he can try an English one. What an opportunity! I keep having to pinch myself."

"What about Rory staying Stateside? I thought that was an option."

"Oh, Garrett, not really, can't you see? He'd be miserable in boarding school, and staying in Applegate? I'm sorry, I know you love the place, but…London. Our son could be experiencing London."

Garrett thought of Rory back in Samantha's barn. "He's really happy here. You should have seen him on the trek."

"How did that go? Was it worth what we paid? And why couldn't I get in touch with you?"

"We had our phones turned off."

"Why?" Her tone of voice said he had to be stark raving mad.

"Rory's big into nature."

"Well, I'm sure we can scrounge up some nature over here."

"Noelle, Rory wants to flip the visitation schedule." There, he'd finally said it.

"I don't understand."

"He wants to live with me and visit you on vacations."

"Over my dead body," his ex snapped back before hanging up on him.

CHAPTER TWELVE

LOOKING FOR A LITTLE PEACE and quiet, a little time alone with just him and the TV remote, Garrett pulled into his driveway only to find Mack sitting on his front stoop. "I hope the camping trip wasn't as bad as the look on your face," his friend called out.

"The aftermath was hell," Garrett replied, getting out of the cruiser.

"The farm remodel? I couldn't watch anymore. That Helena was aptly named. Hell in a handbasket. Red and I could see the whole blowup coming. That's why I took off. Besides, all that money being poured into one house kinda gave me the willies."

Amen. Garrett climbed the steps to unlock the front door. "You want a b—" He caught himself. "You want to see if there's anything to eat?"

"I want a beer," Mack said ruefully. "Can't lie to you, but I'll settle for something to eat. Anything Geneva's laid her hands on. Some of her leftover fried chicken, maybe." He followed Garrett into the empty house. "So, how'd Samantha do with the trail chow? I knew she was nervous about everything being just so."

Garrett scowled. Mack hadn't said *boo* for months, and now he wouldn't shut up. "Rory said he had a great birthday, and that's what counts."

"But?"

"No buts."

"So why are you so touchy?"

He headed for the kitchen and the fridge. "Noelle got a big promotion. In London. She's set on taking Rory with her."

Mack whistled low. "Rory's only mentioned the possibility of boarding school after eighth grade. And I know he wasn't hot on that idea. What are you going to do about London?"

"First I'm going to use the summer to try and make Noelle see reason. Then, if necessary, I'm going to fight her on this."

"You better get yourself one kick-ass lawyer."

Didn't he know it. Trouble was, kick-ass lawyers charged kick-ass fees. Maybe he should just ask Samantha's father for a recommendation. The guy obviously ran in moneyed circles.

"Tell me," he said, pulling fried chicken and sweet tea out of the refrigerator, "what you know about Samantha's family."

"Nothing. Why do you ask?"

He ignored the question. "She doesn't have the same last name as her parents."

"Maybe the guy's her stepfather. Maybe she was married before she moved here. There could be several reasons, but why do any of them matter?"

Garrett poured two glasses of tea, then removed the plastic wrap from the cold chicken. The men ate at the counter, standing up, Mack eyeing him.

"What?" Garrett glowered at his friend. "Can't I ask a few questions? I spent twenty-four hours with the woman, yet I know less about her now than I did yesterday."

Mack tossed a drumstick bone in the garbage under the sink. "I don't believe you. What was she like on the trail?"

"Nice. Although she's obviously not crazy about guns and she doesn't know squat about tents…she's really attuned to animals, kids and nature. And she's drop-dead gorgeous in the morning."

"What more do you need to know?"

"Where she came from. What she's doing here. Whether she's the real deal or—"

"Believe me, Samantha's the real deal." The expression on Mack's face was of absolute certainty. "She doesn't say, but you can tell she's known pain. But now there's a—how can I describe it?—a peace about her. Pretty powerful stuff. She got through to me when no one else could. Made me want to stand where she was standing." Mack suddenly looked sheepish. "You had to be there."

"Your situation's one thing, and I'm glad she helped you out. But I kind of need to know more."

"Because Rory's working for her." Mack reached for more chicken.

"Y-yeah."

Realization dawned on his friend. "Because you're interested in her. Of course. God, I've been blind."

"Believe me it's going nowhere."

"Well, it sure won't go anywhere if you start out looking behind her to see who she might have been, instead of looking right at her to see who she is."

"It's not that simple."

"Yes, it is. Tell me one thing. Do you still want me back on the force?"

"Of course."

"You're not going to ask me what threw me into a four-month drunk? Not going to ask me what I might have done over in Iraq?"

"No. That's different than wanting to know about Samantha's background."

"How is it different?"

"Mack, we have history together. I know your family. I know you."

"You knew the boy I was. The man I was. You don't know me now."

"You're not going to tank our friendship that easily. Whoever you are right now, I accept you."

"And I sincerely appreciate it. I bet Samantha would be real pleased if you decided to take her on face value, as well."

Unable to resign himself to that particular leap of faith, Garrett took a long swig of sweet tea.

"And don't go doing any checks on her," Mack warned.

"I already did. Turned up zip."

"Great. Your snooping will sabotage any chance of a relationship before it's even begun."

There wasn't going to be a relationship. With their obvious differences, the chances Garrett might hook up with Samantha were already slim to none.

So why couldn't he let her background alone?

FRESH FROM HER BATH in the claw-foot tub—thank goodness they hadn't replaced that—Samantha lay between Egyptian cotton sheets so cool and so soft she shouldn't have had any trouble drifting off to sleep. But the height of her new bed—there were actual steps to get into it—the smell of paint and the unabated aggravation as a result of her parents' interference drove her to distraction and wakefulness.

She knew her parents thought they were doing something special for her. Their hearts were in the right place. Unfortunately, their hearts were in the five-star hotel world, the Virginia horse-country world, while her heart had come to rest in Applegate.

In Applegate, she didn't need a designer showplace for a house. She didn't need a gourmet kitchen. It was nice to come back to a place to call home, sure, but, if truth be told, she had slept like a baby on an air mattress in a one-man tent, and had eaten the best breakfast of her life, cooked over an open fire.

By a man she couldn't get out of her thoughts.

Garrett McQuire, who'd viewed her mother's makeover and had taken off as if disgusted with the ostentation.

She didn't blame him.

He had to think this might be what she wanted. Needed. And if she knew one thing from her talks with Red it was that Garrett's ex-wife would have fit right into the newly renovated farmhouse. Only if it was her vacation house. As she'd heard it, Noelle McQuire couldn't stand the simple life in Applegate, while Garrett wouldn't give it up. The sight of Helena's handiwork must have really pushed his buttons.

She tossed and turned throughout the night and was glad to get out of bed when she heard Red's rooster crow. There was plenty of time to spare before her AA sponsor came by to pick up Mack and her for their daily meeting. She absolutely needed that support today. The short lunch trek she had scheduled would keep her mind busy for a few hours afterward. It was the prospect of late afternoon and evening, however, when her mother knew she was free, that had her jumpy.

Padding downstairs—the heart pine floors had been sanded, but not yet stained and sealed—too little time, Helena had complained—Samantha felt as if she was in a luxurious B and B. Antiques— some of them *were* family pieces Red had sold— were artfully mixed with very modern furnishings, giving the place a studied eclectic look. A very beautiful but very impersonal look. There was so much white, Samantha despaired of ever flopping down for a rest on any of her new couches after a hard day's work.

In the kitchen she discovered the cooler from yesterday's trek. Red must have brought it in from the barn. She still couldn't believe how he and Rory had taken care of the llamas, the camping equipment and the tack while she was still absorbing the shock of her renovated living space. Lifting the lid, she let out a sigh of disappointment. Inside was the carefully packaged birthday cake she'd intended to serve Rory with lunch. Forgotten and uneaten. It would still be good. She'd have to make sure he got it today at work. But that wasn't the same.

Poor kid. His birthday trek had been quite the hodgepodge. There was no way she was charging Garrett for it.

Actually, there never had been any intention to charge Garrett for it.

Transferring the remaining food from the cooler to the new stainless Sub-Zero refrigerator, she didn't have the heart to fix herself a big breakfast. Instead, she munched a handful of granola and washed it down with a glass of milk, then, grabbing her boots, she headed outside to check on the llamas. Not long afterward she found her way to the top porch step where she turned her back on the new wicker furniture.

It wasn't her sponsor who showed up to drive to the AA meeting, but Mack in Red's truck.

"Get in," he said, leaning from the driver's side to open the passenger door.

"Do you have a license?"

"Yeah. But my truck sits on my parents' farm. I'm considering reregistering it."

"Thinking of rejoining the living?" she asked, getting into the cab.

"You might say that," he replied, easing Red's pickup down her bumpy drive.

He might be thinking of entering the human race again, but Samantha still worried about Mack. There was something he was holding back. As if he didn't trust his own humanity.

"You going to be around later this afternoon?" she asked. "On the trek I forgot to serve Rory his birthday cake. And I made it especially from one of Geneva's recipes. Carrot."

Mack looked sideways at her.

"Oh, come on. It won't kill you. Although I know what you three bunkhouse rats think of my cooking."

"Bunkhouse rats?"

"I think Francis, Douglas and Owen have trademarked the term *coots.* Would you prefer *possums?*"

"That makes Red, Rory and me sound like mascots. And Garrett's already accusing us of forming your backup team."

"He certainly took off quickly yesterday. Is everything all right?"

"I don't know. You tell me."

"My parents really overdid the house makeover," she said evasively. "I could see where someone might look at me, as a result, and think, *spoiled.*"

"Then maybe you need to stand up to your parents—tell 'em exactly what it is you want and don't want, tell 'em to back off, if necessary. Or maybe you ought to stop worrying about what people think."

"The way you do?"

"I'm not a particularly good role model."

"I'm guessing Garrett doesn't see me as a particularly good role model for Rory," she said.

"That's not the problem."

"So you admit there is a problem?"

"I don't know. I've known Garrett since third grade," Mack replied, carefully maneuvering round a particularly sharp turn in the road. "He's what you call a self-made man. But his whole childhood foster-care experience left pretty deep scars. He's got some hang-ups about commitment."

"A lot of men have commitment phobias."

"Garrett's just the opposite, although I don't think he'd admit it. He wants a stable relationship. An intact family."

"Then he must see his divorce as a huge failure on his part."

"Exactly. And now he won't go out on a limb again for anything temporary or insubstantial." He looked over at her.

Did Garrett see her llama operation as temporary, and, worse yet, her as insubstantial? Was Mack trying to warn her off?

"Hey," he said suddenly. "Rory wanted me to talk to you about the road bowling tournament."

"What about it?" She was still trying to get her

mind around their conversation about Garrett. "I thought he and Red were forming a team."

"They are. But Rory wants to up the odds of a Whistling Meadows victory. He wants you and me to compete."

"And you'd do it?" This was not the Mack she'd come to know.

"Sure. It'll make my godson happy." He grimaced. "And it might just get my best friend off his can."

What was going on? Samantha felt strangely like Alice down the rabbit hole.

FRANCIS, DOUGLAS AND OWEN WERE sitting across from the county courthouse, on a bench under a live oak, out of the afternoon sun. As Garrett descended the courthouse steps, the three retirees waved him over.

"What can you tell us about Cameron Lawrence?" Douglas asked.

"He's Samantha Weston's father. You know Samantha, she bought—"

"Whistling Meadows. Yeah, yeah, we know. That's old news. That and her mother gussying up the place."

That was *old* news? It had happened yesterday.

Owen leaned forward from his seat on the bench. "And don't tell us about Lawrence snooping around the land management office. We know all about that, too."

"Then you know what I know," Garrett replied.

"Oh, come on." Francis looked doubtful. "You went on a camping trip with her…" Did everybody know about that? "Surely she said something about her father's intentions hereabouts."

The strange thing about conversations with Samantha was that they never revealed anything about her or her parents. She'd talk about llamas, the Whistling Meadows' day-to-day operation, Rory's job performance and even Mack, but she always deflected talk of herself. And here Garrett, as sheriff, had considered himself an expert at getting to the facts.

"What we really wanna know," Francis continued, "is if this Lawrence fella is all talk and no action."

"All hat and no cattle," Douglas added.

"I don't know," Garrett admitted.

"Well, don't you think you ought to find out?" Owen exclaimed. "Before he buys up all the available land and turns it into—God forbid—one of those highfalutin' gated retirement communities. What are we payin' you for, son?"

Some days he wondered.

After leaving the three men more riled up than when he'd found them, he stopped to check his phone messages before heading to his office. There were seven voice mails from Noelle.

Although he didn't have the stomach for a go-round with her over Rory's future, she would be the one to know about the Lawrences. From high school on, she'd followed the rich and famous in print and television tabloids.

Feeling not a little sleazy, he punched in her number. She took a while to answer, and when she did, he could hear the sounds of a party or a bar in the background.

"Hello?" She sounded tipsy. "Garrett? Wait! Let me go to the restroom—pardon me, the loo." For a few minutes there were odd voices, miscellaneous sounds and then Noelle's voice, clearer now. "I hope you didn't interrupt my evening to argue with me about Rory."

"No." This wasn't the battle he'd chosen today. "I need some information."

"Yes?"

"Does the name *Cameron Lawrence* ring a bell?"

"Of course. He's only the founder of Ashley International Hotels named for his daughter and heir apparent. The thing is she was arrested for driving under the influence and sent to some secret rehab location. Since then she's dropped out of sight. Very mysterious. Who'd want to give up that lifestyle?"

Apparently, Samantha.

Garrett didn't know whether to dismiss her as wildly irresponsible...or protect her.

CHAPTER THIRTEEN

"DAD, WHAT ARE YOU AND MOTHER really doing here?" Samantha lay sprawled on a porch settee while her father sat sharply erect, reading the *Washington Post*. She knew he wanted a scotch on the rocks but wouldn't indulge in front of her. Helena was in the house, presumably tweaking the decor. An impending thunderstorm made the air heavy.

Her father lowered the paper. "We're taking a little break. The opening of the Singapore Ashley was exhausting. But not as exhausting, I'm afraid, as the building of it. You did a wonderful job."

"Thank you."

"I wish—"

"Dad, don't go there. Please."

"I just wanted to say it's okay that you're taking a breather, too."

"Applegate isn't just a breather. I think it's where I'm supposed to be."

"It's too early to tell," her father replied with conviction. "That's why Dr. Kumar prescribed a year's rest. Don't be too hasty to ink in the rest of your life."

Was that what she was doing? Were her feelings— the attractions she felt—any less valid because she'd placed herself in a new situation?

"Did I ever tell you my father wanted me to be a surgeon?" Cameron continued. "He was a shoe salesman, but he had big dreams for me. I could no more have been a surgeon than I could have flown, and I broke his heart."

"Is that what—?"

"You have a visitor," her father said, looking over her shoulder, an edge to his voice.

She looked up to see Garrett getting out of his cruiser and suddenly felt the way you did when trying to get into a canoe. With one foot on solid ground, the other in a very precarious position.

"Samantha. Mr. Lawrence," he said, mounting the porch steps. "Excuse me, but is Rory working late? He's not at home, and there's no note."

"They must have lost track of time," Samantha replied as she sat up. "He and Red went up Russert's Mountain to take care of the graffiti."

"What graffiti?" Cameron asked.

"Just a little vandalism," Samantha said, not wanting to get into it. Not wanting her father to fix her problems. "No big deal."

"But vandalism? On *your* land?"

"Yes." Uh-oh. This was the proverbial can of worms. Private property, in her father's mind, was sacrosanct. To be protected at all cost.

He turned to Garrett. "I assume this is something my daughter reported to you."

"I know about it."

She could have hugged Garrett for failing to divulge more than that, but she knew her steamroller father. He wouldn't stop until he had the full story. "Dad, look…the guy on the next farm isn't happy I've fenced my pastureland. It cuts off his easy access to the trails his boys used to use. We think the kids might have been acting out their father's displeasure."

"But if this Russert's Mountain is your property, and you're fenced, how did someone manage to get up there?" Cameron was not a man to give up.

"The fencing doesn't go around all sixty acres, Dad."

"Besides, there are roundabout access points," Garrett explained. "If you're determined."

"And why would these people be so determined?"

"Because," Samantha replied, becoming exasperated, "they think they can drive me off Whistling Meadows with their adolescent games. Garbage in the pastures. Damaged f—"

As her father's whole body language took on a

battle readiness, Samantha realized she'd said way too much. "As I said, it's not a big deal."

"It's a very big deal," her father snapped back. "This operation of yours is an investment. And you never let anyone threaten your investments. Haven't I taught you anything?" He turned on Garrett. "What are you doing about this?"

"Dad, it's under investigation." Samantha stood up between the two men. "Garrett, could I have a word with you?" She motioned toward the cruiser.

"Sure," he replied, although she could tell he'd relish staying put and going toe-to-toe with her father.

She gave him a little nudge toward the steps. Big mistake. Although he moved, she was left with the impression of his warm, hard body. Glancing over her shoulder as they headed toward the car, she saw her father watching them, his eyes narrowed.

"Sorry about my father," she said, taking Garrett's arm and leading him not to his cruiser but around the house and across to the barn. Out of sight.

"He's right, you know. About your investment."

"Of course, I know," she replied, stepping into the cool, sweet-smelling barn. Through the doorway she could see tall cumulonimbus clouds massing on the horizon. The atmosphere was humid and filled with electricity. She ran her palm up her neck, lifting her hair, trying for a breath of air. "But I don't need him handling the farm for me. My father will eventually go away. Tanner won't. It would be far wiser to use a little tact with my neighbor. A little patience. None of which my father possesses."

"He would have shot the rattlesnake."

"In a heartbeat." She didn't know who had her more hot and bothered, her father—one way—or Garrett—quite another.

As thunder rumbled in the distance, Garrett scowled. "When did Rory and Red leave?"

"A few hours ago."

"On foot?"

"No. They took this contraption the two of them built. A hybrid. Kind of a cross between a golf cart and an ATV. Red will know enough to get Rory off the mountain before a storm comes, won't he?"

"He should. He's lived here all his life. Knows the mountains and the weather inside out. I trust him."

"Maybe I should be more proactive with Rory," she said, leaning up against a stall and watching the dark purple clouds roil the sky framed by the barn door opening.

"How do you mean?"

"He comes to work. He does his work. Then he hangs out with Red and Mack. Maybe I should supervise his activity more."

"No. That's Noelle's style. Micromanagement."

Garrett reached out to brush a tendril of hair from her face. "I like how you let Rory explore. Work hard. Make decisions for himself."

"You do?" Suddenly, the air in the barn seemed very close.

"Yeah. You don't coddle him." Putting his hand on the timber behind her, he leaned in just as her Black-Berry vibrated. If Rory and Red hadn't been up on the mountain, she would have let the darn thing go to voice mail.

Instead she answered, to Rory's voice. "Samantha? I left a message for Dad, and I'm calling you to say we're okay. We're in an old cabin on the back of the mountain. Red said you might not even know you owned it. It's kinda run-down, but the roof doesn't leak. It's raining like crazy up here."

"Do you want to talk to your dad? He's right beside me."

"Just tell him we're safe," he said as the reception began to break up. "We'll come down when the storm passes."

"Will do." She hung up. "That was Rory. They're in a cabin—"

"On the other side of the mountain. I'd forgotten that place. When we were kids, Mack and I used to take shelter there in bad weather. I'm glad Rory thought to call."

"He said he left a message on your phone, too."

"Wow. Thirteen and turning responsible. Who'd have thought?"

"You've done a good job raising him."

He winced.

Lightning and a clap of thunder directly overhead preceded a downpour by only seconds. It was as if a veil had been dropped over the doorway. The rain hit the yard outside so hard it sprayed and splattered several feet into the interior.

Garrett pushed her farther into the barn. "Where are the llamas?"

"They'll take shelter under the lean-to."

"Then it's just us."

"It's just us."

Before she could take in the full import of that statement, her BlackBerry vibrated again. Without thinking, she picked up the call. "Rory?"

"No, darling, it's your mother. Where are you?"

"In the barn."

"With the llamas?"

"With the sheriff."

"Do you think that's a good idea?"

"Mother…. I'll see you when the rain stops."

Sometimes technology was more aggravation than it was worth.

Watching Samantha, Garrett wondered just how

much it bothered Helena that her daughter was consorting with the locals.

"Everything okay?" he asked when she rang off.

"Of course." She pocketed the BlackBerry, then crossed her arms and walked to stand not far from the doorway, where the rain was still coming down in sheets.

The crazy moment of possibilities had passed. Perhaps he'd better seize the moment of reckoning. It wasn't likely she'd try to escape in this downpour. "Is your real name Ashley?" he asked.

"I prefer to be called Samantha," she replied, her voice becoming guarded.

"Is Samantha a middle name?"

She turned to level her intriguing hazel eyes at him. "Does it matter?"

It shouldn't. But it did. To him. Maybe because, growing up, a name was all he'd had to define himself. One of the conditions of his divorce had been that he'd let Noelle have custody of Rory most of the time if she'd swear to keep the last name McQuire, unless she remarried. Keep the name for Rory. So that he would have a strong sense of family. Of belonging.

When Garrett realized Samantha was staring at him, he shook off thoughts of the past. "It's just that I've known you—what?—a couple weeks Rory's been working for you?—and I know nothing about you."

"You did a background check, if I recall." Right before his eyes she was becoming the cool, distant woman who'd lunched in his office. "And I came up clean."

Thinking of his most recent conversation with Noelle, he felt a guilty knot in his stomach.

"I have nothing to hide," she said. "What do you want to know?"

"Does your father own Ashley International Hotels?"

"Yes." She looked away from him, toward the barn entrance and the rain. In the dim light her fine features were etched with a certain weariness. "I was supposed to take over the business."

Now that surprised him. Noelle made it sound as if Lawrence's daughter's only function was to inherit the family fortune.

She sighed. "You might as well have the whole truth."

Suddenly, he didn't want to know everything. It seemed like an invasion of her privacy. It wasn't as if he was tracking a public enemy.

"I couldn't cut it as a hotelier," she continued in a voice that sounded like a recording. "Oh, I was efficient. I was on top of things. I knew the business from bottom to top. But it was just a job. I wasn't like my father. Hotels didn't define me.

More to the point, the corporate pressures were killing me inside."

An overwhelming sense of protectiveness filled him, making him step toward her. But she raised her hand to ward him off.

"In a business such as ours," she said, "socializing is a very important part. So I rationalized the drinking. I didn't realize—no, I didn't want to admit—that it was a crutch. It smoothed the rough edges of fear."

"You said you knew the ropes. What did you fear?"

"Disappointing my parents." She looked up at him, and he could see tears in her eyes. "I'm their only child. They've poured their hopes and dreams into me."

When he took her in his arms, she let him embrace her. Shield her. He wondered at the inequity of the world. He'd had no hopes and dreams poured into him—nothing beyond minimal expectations—and here she'd had a crushing amount.

"Your parents obviously haven't been slouches in the achievement department," he said, stroking her hair. "They don't need you to fulfill their dreams. They need to let you find your own path."

She wiped her eyes and pushed away from him. "Oh, I think yesterday was a prime example of how well they're able to mind their own business."

"I get the impression they don't think Applegate is any place for an heiress."

She shivered. "Don't use that awful word."

"Okay. But tell me…did you choose Applegate specifically to get a rise out of your parents?"

"No!" Staring out into the lessening rain, she seemed to be deliberating. Finally, she turned to him. "I'm not, by nature, a secretive person, and secrets have a way of getting out in the open, anyway."

This was what he'd been waiting for, so now why did he feel as if he'd bullied her into the telling?

She sat down on a bale of hay. Looked at her hands. "When it became more and more clear that I was not cut out to be a hotelier, I would often rely on alcohol for the courage to face what needed to be done. In the past couple years, I'd had some traffic violations. Several speeding tickets. A fender bender. But my father was able to make them go away…until the last time."

Garrett tried to keep an open mind, but one of his hot buttons had always been the corruptible power of money. But this was Samantha, whom he'd grown to respect. To like. Really like. In order not to say anything judgmental, he said nothing.

Frowning, she continued. "I'd just had lunch and several martinis to give me strength to get through the afternoon. An important meeting. Usually, when I drank, I'd call for a limo, but I was running late. I got in my car, and…I…rear-ended a loaded school bus." She looked up at him, her eyes dry this time but brimming with remorse. "I was the only one seriously hurt, but my nightmares are filled with what-ifs."

His first thought was that there were maybe thirty Rorys on that bus, and this woman—this woman of privilege—had thoughtlessly put innocent lives in jeopardy for—what?—a business meeting.

"You're disgusted," she said softly.

Yes. He was. As a sheriff he dealt in black and white. Right and wrong. Innocence and guilt. How could he not feel righteous disgust?

But from the first time he'd met her, Samantha had proved herself a more subtle matter. A more challenging subject. In her there were shades of gray. Hot and cold running together. Openness and mystery existing side by side. What she'd done appalled him, yes. Until he thought of the strength it must have taken to make this confession. To divulge something she clearly hadn't wanted to tell him. Even Mack, since Iraq, hadn't been this honest with him.

Garrett thought of Samantha's pain. Of trying to be shoehorned into a life that was not a fit. "No," he replied, at last, extending his hand to her. "I'm not disgusted."

She took his hand as if she was about to shake and say goodbye. "As a sheriff, you know the rest, I'm sure. After I was released from the hospital, I had to appear before a judge."

"Who first took away your license."

"Yes."

"And then sentenced you to community service." His heart sank, and he removed his hand from hers. "Don't tell me Whistling Meadows is your community service."

"No. Whistling Meadows is the direct result of rehab. Actually, it's been a continuation of rehab."

The rain had stopped as abruptly as it had begun, and, as happened so often with these mountain storms, the sun was shining brightly through still-dark and ominous clouds, catching the dust motes floating in the barn's air, making them sparkle. The only sound was the drip of rain off the eaves, the call of songbirds emerging from shelter. And the pounding in his ears.

He didn't know what to do with this new information about Samantha. It wasn't what he expected. He knew she attended AA. He knew she didn't have a license. But to buy up sixty acres of prime real estate as rehab? To keep her hands busy? People around here took up woodworking, rock climbing, gardening. Clearly, Samantha's lifestyle was too rich for his blood.

"Darling?" Helena Lawrence appeared in the barn doorway. "Ruggiero's come back for us. You need to hurry and dress. Remember, the Atwaters have flown in to have dinner with us at the inn." She eyed Garrett dismissively. "Reservations are for eight-thirty."

He didn't need that little extra reminder of the social gulf between Samantha and himself. "I need to call Rory," he said. "To make sure he and Red are okay." With barely a nod for both women, he left.

CHAPTER FOURTEEN

AS SHE WATCHED GARRETT WALK away, Samantha tried not to show any emotion, tried not to give her mother any hint of the inner turmoil that had her stomach tightening. Garrett had said he wasn't disgusted by her disclosure, but his body language had said otherwise. What had he wanted from her? As a lawman was he thinking she needed punishment, not rehab? Did he see her as a frivolous socialite? It stunned her that *his* good opinion of *her* mattered.

Helena, whose goal was to make life as beautiful and as problem-free as possible, could always sense disruption in her family's private universe. "What's wrong?" she asked. "Why was the sheriff still here?" By the stiff tone, Samantha could tell her mother clearly did not consider Garrett part of and party to the Lawrence circle.

"We're concerned for Rory and Red." That was certainly no lie. "They're still on the mountain."

"Well, I'm sure the sheriff can handle it. He has a

whole department at his disposal if necessary." Her mother reached out to finger a lock of Samantha's hair, which had gone very curly with the humidity. "Darling, when did you stop straightening your hair? It's so…unruly. You must let me make an appointment for you with Vivica at the inn."

"Mother, please, stop. I like my hair natural." If she could be honest with Garrett and survive having him walk away from her, maybe, just maybe, she could get up the courage to be straight with her mother. "And I'm sorry, but I won't be having dinner with you tonight."

"But the Atwaters—"

"I've never liked the Atwaters. Damien can't keep his hands to himself."

Helena's eyes grew wide. She looked as if she feared Samantha might be about to have a meltdown. "We don't want to stress you."

"Frankly, I am stressed, and we need to talk about why."

"The sheriff, of course. He shouldn't have worried you about his son."

"*My* employee." Her young knight in shining armor. "Mother…I'm not talking about the sheriff's family. I'm talking about ours. I've always tried to be a good daughter—"

"And you have been. The absolute best. Our glittering star. That's why your father and I want to help you put your life back together."

"But it's obvious you're trying to put it back the way it was. Or, at least, to superimpose my old life on top of the new."

Helena appeared confused. "Certainly. What could be wrong with that?"

"I'm not the same woman who entered rehab. I've changed more than my name."

"Please, don't fret about the name change. We understand the temporary need for anonymity while you recuperate."

"You don't understand. Samantha Weston is who I've become. Who I want to be. And not just temporarily."

With the tips of her fingers, her mother brushed Samantha's forehead. "You look tired, darling. Dr. Kumar prescribed rest, yet all I've seen you do is work. And manual labor at that. You have the resources to hire a real staff."

"I love the work. It leaves my body exhausted, and my mind peaceful."

"Darling, that's why God invented Pilates."

"Mother, be serious."

"All right. Maybe it is better if you don't join us tonight. I recommend a long relaxing bath and an early bedtime." She lightly kissed Samantha's cheek.

"But if you need us, we're only a phone call away. Ruggiero can always come get you."

Samantha could not wait for her mother and father to leave the farm—and felt guilty for her traitorous impulses. But her loyalties lay elsewhere. As soon as the limo turned out of her drive and onto the county road, she called Rory's cell phone. Voice mail kicked in. She told herself it might be the iffy reception in the mountains. Or perhaps Rory had turned the phone off to conserve the battery. She could hope. If, however, the guys had run into trouble, she needed to get to them.

Because Garrett had blown up in the aftermath of the spying debacle, she'd promised to look after his son's best interests when he was at Whistling Meadows. Rory wouldn't now be up there somewhere if he hadn't been determined to wipe out the graffiti at the campground. Her campground. She felt a responsibility, especially since she suspected Garrett thought of her as wildly irresponsible.

Checking her watch, she figured there were a couple more hours of daylight. She quickly threw a first aid kit and a high-powered flashlight into her backpack, then pulled on walking boots, grabbed a staff and headed on foot through the outer pasture toward the forest trail. When she passed Tanner Harris's house and saw his boys hitching a trailer to a truck, for the first time ever she wished she had some kind of ATV or dirt bike to cover the ground quickly.

But she was strong, and purposeful hiking was different than an amble with llamas. Despite some muddy spots from the rain, she made good progress up the ridge. She'd be a lot happier, however, if she saw Rory and Red coming at her from the opposite direction. In fact, it struck her that if she didn't meet them by the time she arrived at the campground, she had no idea where this cabin was that Rory spoke of. Before purchasing it, she'd seen her property outlined on a map, but she hadn't explored it all yet. What kind of steward of the land did that make her?

If she was serious about being Samantha Weston, she needed to sit down and rethink her business as a permanent undertaking.

Not far from where Garrett had shot the rattlesnake, along a portion of trail faced on one side by granite outcroppings and on the other by a steep drop off the ridge, Samantha saw Red's homemade ATV. It was empty.

Her heart pounding wildly, Samantha ran the remaining distance. "Rory! Red!"

"Down here!" Red's voice came from below.

"Are you all right?"

"Yeah." Rory didn't sound okay. "I lost my cell phone. We watched it slide right off the cart."

Oh, Garrett was going to love this.

Samantha slipped her backpack off, then cautiously approached the edge of the trail. An almost vertical drop, there wasn't much besides rocks and some scraggly trees to hold on to—and Red and Rory were hanging on for dear life about twenty feet below. She could look down on the tops of their heads. The phone could easily have bounced all the way to the base of the ridge. Even if the terrain were level, the light was going fast. Something as small as a cell phone would be impossible to find.

"Leave it!" she called out. "It's not worth risking life and limb."

"But my mom bought it for me!" Rory wailed. "She's gonna kill me!"

"Not if you get killed here first." The thought of a fall—or snakebite—made her cringe. "Red, talk some sense into him."

"The Duchess is right. I'm not sure I want to die for a cell phone, kid."

"Do you know how hard I had to work to convince her I'd be responsible? Do you know when I'll get another phone? *Never.*" He clung to his tree limb so tightly his knuckles showed white in the fading light.

"Rory," Samantha replied, kneeling by the precipice and using her calmest negotiator's voice. "You lost the phone while doing a difficult job for me.

Under difficult circumstances. I'll call your mother and explain that it's my fault. I'll replace the phone."

"You would do that?"

"Yes." It was only money.

"You're not going get a better offer than that," Red urged.

"Don't tell my dad."

"I won't tell him," she promised.

"Okay, but…now how do I get back up onto the trail?"

"Very carefully," Red cautioned. "I'm gonna stay here and spot you. The Duchess is above if you need a hand up. You all right with that, Duchess?"

"Y-yes." Although she didn't weigh much more than Rory, and there was nothing to grab on to along this side of the trail, there was no question but that she must be strong for this boy who'd risked so much for her. She lay flat on the ground and extended her arms over the edge. Sharp pebbles dug into her stomach. "I'm ready."

Painful seconds passed as Rory made his slow ascent. When he was just beneath her, he looked up, his expression turning from nervous concentration to utter relief. He thrust his hand in hers and held on as if he never planned to let go.

She clung to him and slithered backward on her belly, pulling as he pushed. Finally, he clambered over the edge and flopped next to her, panting.

"Nobody worry about me," a sarcastic voice floated up from below. "This is just a walk in the park for a man my age."

"Red!" With a start both Samantha and Rory turned their attention to getting their friend back to safety. But as they hung over the edge of the trail, arms outstretched, Red proved to be extremely dexterous at finding tree branches and toeholds to make his way up unassisted.

On the trail, however, he rolled onto his back with a grunt. "This isn't how I saw retirement playin' out."

Rory chuckled. "Admit it. You've been bragging to Francis, Douglas and Owen how your old age is five times more exciting than theirs."

"Well, I'm thinkin' of scalin' back the excitement." He sat up on the hard-packed earth. He'd lost his John Deere cap, and his thin, graying hair sticking up in wisps about his head, along with his sunburned cheeks and nose, gave him the look of an angry imp. "Let's get home. I need some Ben-Gay."

They all stood. "I don't know what to say," Samantha said, bending to put on her backpack, "except to apologize to both of you. You've been nothing but helpful, yet what have your efforts gotten you? Scrapes and bruises and not much else."

Red took the backpack out of her hands. "Eh. What else do I have to do with my time?" His tone was gruff, but there was a twinkle in his eye. "C'mon, there's room for all three of us to ride."

Samantha pulled out her BlackBerry and offered it to Rory. "Your father's probably wondering why he's being routed to voice mail. Call him and let him know you're okay."

Rory did but fudged an explanation as to why he was calling on Samantha's phone. Garrett promised to be waiting at the farm.

Samantha was glad of the lift. It was definitely time to follow her mother's advice with a long soaking bath and an early bedtime. But best-laid plans…

When they pulled into the barnyard, the cruiser was parked near the paddock fence, but there was no sign of Garrett. Nor any sign of the llamas. The inner-pasture gate was wide open. Dread began to form in the pit of Samantha's stomach.

"What the—?" Red pulled his ATV to a halt near the barn just as Garrett came around the farmhouse, leading Ace by his halter. The llama's white coat showed ghostly in the gathering darkness.

"What happened?" Samantha asked, jumping out of the cart and running to Ace.

"I don't know," Garrett replied. "When I got here, the gate was open. This one was grazing on the new flowers next to the porch. I've put out a call to be on the lookout for the others."

In the beam of the barn's spotlight, Samantha checked Ace all over. He seemed fine. Only a little miffed that he'd been pulled from his smorgasbord. She breathed a sigh of relief. "One down, five to go."

Garrett began to lead the llama back to the pasture.

"Let's not put him in there yet," Samantha decided. "We'll shut him in the paddock next to the barn." If someone had let the llamas out, they could have tampered with the pasture itself. Until she could be certain, she wanted her herd safe.

When Ace was secured to her satisfaction, she turned to find Garrett, Rory and Red waiting. "You're going to help find the others?"

"Did you think we'd leave you to fend for yourself?" Garrett asked. She could have kissed him.

"I'll take Rory in my truck," Red offered. "You two go in the car."

"When you find the boys, don't chase them," Samantha warned, worry making her voice crack. She passed out leads and, remembering Rory had no phone, slipped Red her BlackBerry, reminding herself to buy walkie-talkies for the farm. "Take some feed with you," she urged. "As you approach them, act as if it's no big deal they're out. We don't want to frighten them."

She thought about how her own fear had moderated once she discovered she wasn't alone in this crisis.

Scooping grain into his pockets, Garrett noted again the automatic concern Samantha showed for her livestock. Not, it seemed, as an investment, but as living creatures under her care. Surely, she wasn't faking that consideration.

"We'll find them," he assured her as they got in the cruiser. "Are they microchipped?"

"Yes." She looked straight ahead. "I'm always so careful to lock the gates."

"Don't beat yourself up," he said, following Red's taillights down the drive toward the county road. "Could the llamas open the gate by themselves?"

"They're clever enough to. That's why the latches are special."

At the end of her drive, Red turned his truck left, so Garrett headed right. Toward Tanner Harris's. He had to ask. "Do you think—?"

"It's crossed my mind. When I was crossing the outer pasture to find Rory and Red, I spotted his sons. They saw me leaving the farm." She took a deep breath. "I hate to think they'd stoop so low."

This had gone on long enough. When the llamas had been rounded up, he was going to make her sit down and file a formal complaint.

As he turned onto the Tanner property, the dogs began howling, but there were no other signs of life. The lights were off in the house, and Tanner's truck, trailer and ATVs were gone. The guy was probably out cementing his alibi.

"Don't get out," he warned as Samantha opened the passenger door. He switched on the dashboard spotlight and fanned the property. Junk spread out across the yard, and the dogs tied to the tree were the only living things highlighted in the intense beam. The barking and growling had reached an earsplitting level.

"With the dogs here," Samantha said, "I don't think the boys would venture in this direction. Can we drive back along my frontage and train the light on the property across the road?"

"Sure." He turned the cruiser around. "I'll drive. You man the spotlight."

"Llamas are so curious, and there's so much vegetation that's poisonous to them," she said with a catch in her voice. "Rhododendron, skunk cabbage, milkweed—"

"Samantha, stop. Don't make trouble where there is none."

"You're right. But if this had happened in rehab, I'd be off llama duty and back to latrines."

He drove slowly close to the shoulder, straining to catch a glimpse of her animals. He wasn't a religious man, but he said a prayer that they found them before a predator did. He wanted desperately to keep her spirits up. "If you quit blaming yourself," he said, "I'll let you in on a fact of life around here. At least once a week the sheriff department's called upon to round up escaped livestock. Ask Red to tell you about the time he tried raising goats."

As she trained the beam beyond the roadside, she sat forward on the seat with her nose almost on the windshield. "You're not just saying that to make me feel better."

Sort of. "No. Farmers around here have a lot invested in their animals. But even the most experienced of them get it wrong sometimes. Farming's hard and by no means foolproof."

"Call me sentimental, but the boys aren't just livestock to me."

The other farmers in the area might call her sentimental, but he called her kindhearted. Among other qualities, equally distracting.

"Over there!" she cried. Halfway up a gentle slope almost directly across from her drive were three forms that, without the spotlight, might have been mistaken for bales of hay. "It's Humvee, Fred and Mephisto."

When he stopped the cruiser, Samantha got out slowly. "Wait here," she said.

Her extended hands full of grain, she advanced on the llamas through the tall grass, making a soft kissing sound as she went. The llamas seemed almost relieved to see her and accepted the grain readily. She hooked leads to their halters, then walked them back to the cruiser as he tried to call Rory.

"I keep getting voice mail," he complained as Samantha leaned into the open window.

"Red has my phone—the number is 555-6881. I'm going to walk these three home."

He didn't call right away. Instead he allowed himself the luxury of a few seconds watching her lead the boys across the road. Woman and beasts swayed in a slow, sensuous rhythm as the fireflies began their evening dance above her head. When she disappeared out of the arc formed by his headlights, he wondered if the feeling of longing that rose hot inside him was real. Or if she'd bewitched him.

He added her phone number to his listings before calling. Red answered. "We have Mr. Jinx. He was in Isolde Stone's kitchen garden. Scared her nearly to death. Lucky he didn't get shot. We got him in Jonathan's horse trailer, and he's going to drive him back to Whistling Meadows."

"We found Humvee, Fred and Mephisto," Garrett replied. "So that leaves Percy unaccounted for."

"We'll keep looking. Call if you find him."

Garrett drove up Samantha's drive to tell her the latest. By the time he pulled into the yard, the four llamas were safely in the paddock next to the barn and

Samantha was latching the gate. "They're bringing Mr. Jinx home," he said, getting out of the cruiser.

He'd hoped to see more relief on her face. "I don't know where Percy could be," she replied. "He's such a homebody. Do you suppose…" she seemed to grow smaller before his eyes "…someone *took* him?"

"Don't even think it." He wrapped an arm around her shoulders to steady her. "We're not finished searching. I don't know about you, but I need a drink of water before we head out again." He was more concerned about her well-being. "You need to stay hydrated, too."

She seemed to resist, but he propelled her toward the back of the house. Together, they climbed the steps to the kitchen door. He was distressed to find she'd left the house open. Most residents did around here, but then they hadn't had a growing spate of unpleasant incidences aimed at them. He went ahead and opened the screen door, then felt the wall for the light switch.

In the middle of the kitchen stood Percy, blinking. He'd opened all the cupboards and had strewn the contents about the room. Right now he was finishing the last of a package of Fig Newtons.

CHAPTER FIFTEEN

WHY—NOW—DID HER KNEES GO WEAK? As Percy cast a haughty long-lashed look that seemed to chastise them for their late arrival at his party, Samantha slumped against Garrett and felt uncontrollable laughter bubble up from deep within her. She clung to him and didn't care that he might think she'd lost it. She felt such relief.

And such an unexpected sense of belonging.

This was her house—the new decor had now been christened, personalized. These were her llamas. Her naughty boys. And her new friends had helped her round them up. Keep them safe. Her friends, to whom she felt a rising sense of commitment.

As her laughter died down to a few intermittent giggles, Garrett supported her in the strong circle of his arms. Oh, my. His chest was so firm and warm against her cheek, it was tempting to close her eyes and dwell in the pure physical moment. But she had to ask herself, was what she felt toward him friendship alone? She looked up and found him staring at her with amusement shot through with longing.

"I'm not going bonkers, I promise," she declared, trying to explain her giddiness. "I'm just so relieved. I couldn't stop worrying about Rory and Red up on the mountain during the storm."

"I should be angry with you for going after them and risking your own safety."

Aw, he would worry about her? Everything seemed so laughably absurd. Except the steady beat of Garrett's heartbeat beneath the palm of her hand.

"Then…then I was so anxious about my AWOL boys." She glanced over at Percy, who'd settled into a *kush* position in the middle of the messy kitchen floor and was now humming serenely. "Rory and Red…and you were wonderful to help me. I can't thank you enough."

"You can thank me by locking your doors when you take off."

She patted his chest. "Always the sheriff."

"Not this time, Samantha." Her name on his lips was quiet. And intimate. And made her push away from him because she suddenly wanted him too much. In a way that would threaten the vulnerable nature of her new identity. Suddenly, the silliness of the situation evaporated, replaced by an unseen spark and sizzle.

He drew her back to him. "What's going on between us?" His question was little more than a sensuous growl.

"You don't know, either?"

"Damned if I do. Yet whatever it is, it's keeping me awake nights."

His admission made her smile. "Me, too."

"But I have a feeling you have more on your mind at the moment than starting up a new relationship." He had to be thinking of her admission earlier in the barn. "And my life's not exactly free and clear right now."

"Rory," she said.

"Yeah. Custody issues. His mother's determined to take him with her to London."

"Permanently?"

"Until she gets her next big promotion." The look in his eyes grew hard, and Samantha could see the intimate moment slipping away.

Perhaps, considering her own situation, that was for the best. "Speaking of Rory," she said, "you should call him to tell him we've found Percy."

She expected him to step away from her, but he didn't. Instead, his large hands rested lightly on her shoulders. He looked at her as if he might be trying to read her mind.

"You're right," he said abruptly.

She made the first move to part. "I'll take Percy to join the others."

By the time Red and Rory pulled into the barnyard ahead of Jonathan Stone with Mr. Jinx in his trailer, Samantha had the other boys secured for the night in the paddock, and Garrett appeared to have his emotions firmly under lock and key.

Thanking everyone profusely, Samantha offered cold lemonade, but only Rory seemed inclined to accept.

"No thanks," Garrett said for the two of them and urged his son toward the cruiser. "We need to head out. I have to pick up some papers at the office before we turn in." His manner was all business now, and Samantha couldn't catch his eye.

Red was the last to go. "You and the sheriff have a falling out?"

"I—I don't think so. Although he didn't like the fact I'd left the house unlocked."

Red chuckled.

"What?" Samantha had begun to suspect Red viewed the activity at Whistling Meadows as some entertaining reality show.

"Nothin'. Nothin' I couldn't have seen comin'. Good night, Duchess." With a backward wave, he hobbled up to the bunkhouse.

She looked in on the llamas in the paddock once

more, doubled-checked the latch on the gate, then glanced at tomorrow's schedule in the barn. A short trek to Lookout Rock with a group of junior boys from Camp Oseegee. An easy day. Which she suddenly craved. Now a brief shower would have to substitute for that long bath. Those Egyptian cotton sheets beckoned. And, maybe, dreams of how reassuring a certain sheriff's heartbeat had felt beneath her cheek.

Trying to keep it real, she did a quick cleanup of Percy's mess in the kitchen before heading upstairs. If she let him, he'd adapt to being a house pet. No sooner had she stepped into the shower, than there came an awful banging at her front door. Her first thought was of Red or Mack. Shutting off the water and wrapping herself in a terry robe, she hurried downstairs only to find Garrett on her porch, his face clouded with anger.

When she opened the door, he stepped inside, unasked. "What the hell do you think you're doing, buying my son a new cell phone?"

Samantha clasped the robe tightly about her. "He lost his on the mountain."

"*He* lost it. *He* will earn the money to replace it. I don't need you aiding and abetting irresponsible adolescent behavior."

She ignored the insult. "It may take him all summer to earn the money. He's only getting paid for four hours a day at minimum wage."

"Then it will take all summer."

"Until then, what will he use for a phone?" Irritated by his intractability, Samantha tossed her head, and water droplets flew all over the hardwood floor and the sheriff's uniform. "I think it's clear the phone's proven its usefulness as a safety device."

"He'll just have to curb his activities. Stay where he can be reached without a phone."

"Essentially, you're grounding him."

"Those are the logical consequences of his actions, sure. Kids screw up. Parents correct them."

"Because," she said, speaking slowly to contain her growing exasperation, "his actions were a result of his job—he was up on the mountain, getting rid of the graffiti at *my* campsite—I felt responsible. I offered to replace the phone."

"When a deputy loses a piece of department equipment, he or she pays for the replacement. As you can imagine, the policy's very effective at deterring loss."

"But we're not talking about deputies. We're talking about your son."

"All the more reason to teach responsibility early on. Besides, do you know how much it costs to replace that particular phone?"

"I have an idea. But it's no big deal." As soon as she'd said the words, she realized she'd made a huge mistake.

Garrett sucked in his breath. Samantha couldn't know how those three words—*no big deal*—got him riled.

"I guess that's where you and I differ," he replied, keeping his frustration in check. "On a fundamental level. To me, life is a big deal right down to the details." He looked around the newly decorated room. "But, of course, you wouldn't understand that concept."

"What does that mean?" Scowling, she stood tall, which didn't seem very tall at all, considering she was barefoot and barely came to his chin.

For the first time since he'd barged into her house, he noticed her hair was damp. He tried not to think that he'd pulled her from a shower. With the prospect that she had nothing on under the robe, thoughts of her as a spoiled heiress were replaced by thoughts of her as the soft and alluring woman who'd been in his arms less than an hour ago. He shouldn't be having this conversation. Not here. Not now.

"Are you going to stand there and glower at me," she asked, crossing her arms over the front of her robe, creating a very distracting gap. "Or are you going to explain what you mean?"

"Everything's easy for you," he said as he threw a hand out to indicate the expensive surroundings. "You buy an old farmhouse, and in a twenty-four-hour span you have something out of *Architectural Digest*."

"That was my mother's doing, and you know it. I liked the house just the way it was."

"That's not the point. Money is. I always get an uneasy feeling when people start throwing it around."

"Ah. Does my family have wealth? Yes. There, I've admitted our 'dirty little secret.' Do we waste our resources? Definitely not. My father didn't become a successful self-made man by squandering his money."

Her candor took him aback.

"I want to compensate Rory for the phone he lost," she continued. "Will you let me or not?"

"No."

FOR SEVERAL DAYS, when Samantha ran errands in town, she expected to see Garrett around every corner. By the fourth day, she knew he was avoiding her.

Just as well.

She certainly didn't want to pursue the topic he'd unexpectedly cracked open before the blowup. In the kitchen. The topic of attraction. Illogical attraction. And mutual, it had seemed. Until their fight. What a stupid fight. While she'd dealt with guys who were drawn to her because of her money, she'd never come across a guy who was repulsed by it.

She'd just bet if she called Dr. Kumar, he'd tell her it was too early to begin a relationship, anyway. She had other things to deal with. Avoiding stressful situations being on top of the list.

Garrett.

And her parents came to mind.

As she'd seen more and more of her mother— Helena kept busy applying the finishing touches on her "housewarming gift," which was now her official title for the extreme-makeover home invasion, and, while she was on the subject, how could Samantha be so heartless and ill–brought up as to turn down such a generous present?—her father had seemed to disappear. When he did have the occasional meal with the two women, he was very secretive. A bad sign, usually portending a significant purchase.

"Samantha? Hello? You haven't touched the peach cobbler." Rachel's voice came to her from far away. "Is something wrong with it?"

She blinked and found herself staring into the diner owner's kind face. Glancing down, she discovered the ice cream had already melted in a puddle over the warm, fragrant dessert sitting forgotten on the counter in front of her.

"I was just enjoying a minute to myself," she replied evasively, lifting the spoon and breaking into the crisp crust. It wasn't quite a lie. She'd come into town this afternoon to buy stamps and to place an order for twelve box lunches for tomorrow's trek.

And to escape Helena's decorating frenzy. "Mmm. This cobbler is wonderful."

Rachel gave her a knowing look. "I understand what it's like when visiting kin overstay their welcome. You don't need the excuse of placing an order. Just come in anytime, and I'll let you eat in the storeroom."

"You don't ever offer us the storeroom," Douglas said as he, Owen and Francis plopped themselves down on the stools next to Samantha.

"That's because you want to be right up front," Rachel quipped, automatically pouring three sweet teas. "Where you can see and be seen."

"Speaking of which…" Douglas turned to Samantha. "You seen your pa today?"

"Not yet."

The men looked at each other and grinned.

"What do you know?" Samantha asked, a hard lump joining the cobbler in her stomach.

"If we did know anything," Francis replied, "and I'm not saying we do—we wouldn't *say* anything because we're not gossips."

Rachel snorted indelicately.

"We're not!" Owen declared, an injured look on his face. "We're retired gentlemen. And we don't kiss and tell."

"Nosiree," Douglas added. "We live and let live. Your business is no business of ours."

"Then why did you bring up the subject of my father?" Samantha asked.

"We didn't," Francis sniffed prissily and turned his attention to his iced tea. "We were just asking after him. Neighborly like."

Right.

Samantha didn't need any more surprises. She needed to get home to grill her mother. Wolfing down the rest of her cobbler—oh, wouldn't Helena swoon over that lapse in etiquette?—she paid Rachel, then headed out to the sidewalk and her bike. When she couldn't resist glancing next door at the sheriff's offices, she was startled to see Garrett coming toward her. He was dressed, as usual, in his pressed and starched uniform, but all she could see was the man who had emerged bare-chested from the lake on Russert's Mountain. The summer heat must be getting to her.

She half expected him to tip his Stetson and walk on by. He didn't.

Instead, he stopped in front of her. "Can I have a word with you?"

She was a little disconcerted that she couldn't see his eyes behind his sunglasses. "S-sure."

Without explanation, he escorted her down the sidewalk and across Main Street bustling with Saturday traffic to a gazebo on a little patch of green that served as the town war memorial. Although anyone passing by could see them, their conversation wouldn't be overheard. She wondered why the expression *hiding in plain sight* sprang to mind.

"Okay," she said, once they were alone. "What's on your mind?"

"I'm sorry I flew off the handle the other night."

"Are you going to let me pay for the phone then?"

"No. I don't believe throwing money at a problem solves anything, but, even so, I shouldn't have reacted the way I did."

"As if I were your ex, perhaps? And an automatic adversary?"

"No, I've never confused you with Noelle," he replied. "But maybe her tabloid fascination with the rich and famous prejudiced me toward your situation."

"My situation?"

"Your parents. Their obvious wealth. You."

"That's an interesting prejudice." This was turning into the strangest apology. "Quite frankly, I don't understand you."

"Which was my argument exactly."

She reached up and took off his sunglasses to better read his mood. "What is your real complaint here?"

"We're totally different," he replied, standing stiffly before her, hands on his hips, staring at her with those unsettling blue eyes. "We don't look at life the same way. We don't approach problem solving the same way. In fact, I'd say we come from two separate universes."

"Oh, so we're different?" She frowned at the painful truth. "As in…I'm a recovering alcoholic and you're sober as a judge? As in you have a child and I'm childless? As in you have roots and know who you are, but I'm just beginning to discover my identity? Yes, we're different. I think you were going for the idea that one of us is privileged and one isn't. But who is which?"

He had the good sense to look uncomfortable.

"I'm feeling this vague dislike coming from you," she continued, warming to her subject. "As if you find the person you *think* I might be irresponsible, immature, unattractive, distasteful. I don't really know. At least Tanner Harris dislikes me honestly. Because, the way he sees it, I did something detrimental—something specific—to him and his family."

Garrett startled her by laughing.

"What's so funny?"

"I'm sorry," he said with a grin. "But I'm offended you compared me to Tanner Harris…and Tanner came out on top."

"If the shoe fits—"

"But the biggest joke is that you'd think I dislike you."

"You don't?"

"How could I dislike a woman who had the guts to stand before me in nothing but a robe and damp hair and give me a tongue-lashing?"

She smiled. Perhaps the heady scent of the old-fashioned pink roses climbing the gazebo made her soften. "So you don't consider me a threat to public safety?"

"Never really did."

"How about a dangerously spoiled heiress?"

"Not anymore."

"What made you change your mind?"

He took both her hands in his, then turned them palms up. "For starters, heiresses don't have calluses."

She tossed her head. "And here I thought you were attracted to my wild and wanton, wet tresses."

He didn't smile at her attempt at humor. In fact, his expression was dead serious. And filled with a blatant hunger.

A little startled at her own audacity, she withdrew her hands from his as he suddenly looked over her shoulder. She turned to see her parents' limo coming to a stop alongside the little park.

Her father got out of the back before Ruggiero opened the driver's door. "I'm glad I found the two of you together," Cameron said, climbing the gazebo steps, a sheaf of papers in his hand.

Samantha recognized the take-charge glint in his eye. "What have you been up to, Dad?"

"I took care of your problem." He thrust the documents toward her, but shot Garrett a pointed look. "When it seemed neither you nor the sheriff were going to do anything about it."

With increasing alarm, she stared at the papers in her hand. A bill of sale signed and notarized. Giving her sole ownership of Tanner Harris's property. "Oh, no, what have you done?"

"I made him an offer he couldn't refuse." Her father appeared more puffed up and pleased with himself than usual. "Harris and his family will be out by the end of next week. I don't care what you do with the place. When Dr. Kumar gives you the okay to leave Applegate, donate the combined properties to the town for a park. That would make a helluva tax write-off."

The expression on Garrett's face was unreadable. But she'd bet the twitch of his jaw muscle didn't signify approval.

CHAPTER SIXTEEN

GARRETT'S FIRST IMPULSE WAS TO smash his fist into the middle of Cameron Lawrence's self-satisfied face.

His next thought was the memory of Samantha, all dressed up and looking vulnerable with a bottle of forbidden wine in her hand simply because her overbearing parents had rolled into town for a visit. He needed to protect her. To get her away from the damage they'd now caused. Physical violence wasn't going to help her.

"Well, sweetheart," Lawrence said, engulfing his daughter in a bear hug she clearly didn't appreciate, "our work here is done. The luggage is in the limo, and I'm on my way to the farm to pick up your mother. Nothing left to do but say goodbye. You want a ride?"

As if stunned, Samantha shook her head.

"Don't be long then," he said, casting a smug proprietary glance in Garrett's direction before heading down the steps and into the big black car.

Samantha fairly shook with unexpressed rage. Her

eyes flashing a certain desperation, she threw her hands and the papers into the air. "How old do I look?" she shouted to no one in particular. "Do I have *helpless minor* stamped on my forehead?" Her cheeks aflame, she began to pace the gazebo. "What am I going to do with these people?"

"You're not going to let them get to you. They're leaving."

"And leaving me with a mess. Can you tell me Tanner's not going to spread the word of his windfall? Can you tell me people aren't already regarding me differently because of my parents' actions?"

He couldn't tell her otherwise.

But he could offer her a breather. "Ride your bike back to the farm," he said. "I'd take you, but the exercise will let off some steam. Say goodbye to your parents. Then cancel any trek you might have scheduled for tomorrow."

She scowled. "Are you trying to boss me around, too?"

"No. I promise. I'll explain later."

"This better be good. I'm so angry I could scream. In fact, I think will. All the way up to Whistling Meadows. People might as well start talking now as later."

"Don't worry about other people."

"How much later should I expect your explanation?" she asked, narrowing her eyes at him as if trying to determine if he might be a spy for the enemy.

"Give me a call when your parents are gone."

"Do I dial 9-1-1?" she asked, rolling her eyes.

He unclipped her BlackBerry from her belt and entered his personal cell number.

The stiff outraged set to her shoulders hadn't eased one bit as she grabbed the phone, turned on her heel and sprinted toward Rachel's Diner and her bike, leaving the legal papers strewn over the gazebo floor.

SHE WAS SO EXHAUSTED WITH unresolved fury that Samantha almost hadn't called Garrett after her parents left. What could he possibly do to help? But she'd called her sponsor because she'd really, really wanted a drink. She'd suggested Samantha first listen to what Garrett had to say, then, if the urge to drink was still strong, she'd swing by. There was plenty of time to catch the evening AA meeting in Brevard. So Samantha had phoned the sheriff. To give him a shot at providing a magic solution. He'd told her to be ready with an overnight knapsack and sleeping bag.

When Garrett pulled into her yard, she was perched on the top step of the porch, watching the hummingbirds hover over the newly trellised trumpet vine, reminding herself to breathe, to stay in the moment. At the sound of the cruiser's approach, she looked up and saw that it was towing a trailer loaded with an ATV. Garrett came to a stop at the end of the stone walkway and got out of the car with a poster-sized roll of paper in hand. He was dressed in jeans and a T-shirt.

Not exactly brimming with enthusiasm, she dragged her gear down the steps toward him. "So why did I cancel on tomorrow's customers?"

He unrolled the sheet of paper and spread it out on the hood of his car. "I reckoned you probably couldn't put your finger on your own copy—what with your mother's redo and all—so I borrowed this from the land management office. Because I thought you might like a reminder of who the real Samantha Weston is."

She looked down on a map—not an ordinary map but a surveyor's map of the property, including Whistling Meadows and Russert's Mountain. Her land.

"I know you've groomed the west-side trails to Lookout Rock and the lake," he continued, "but I didn't know if you'd explored some of the old logging roads running along the eastern boundary. Or if you'd had a chance to hike to the cabin Rory and Red took shelter in."

"No, I haven't."

"Then that's what we're going to do."

This was not what she'd expected. She'd anticipated some not-so-patient hand-holding, maybe, while he allowed her to vent. Or an AA–type intervention to keep her from turning to drink. Or maybe a trip to Asheville and the movies as a distraction. But this…this offer cut to the heart of the discoveries she'd begun to make about herself. And where she belonged. He was absolutely the sweetest man.

"So what do you say?"

"I'll have to get at least one llama ready," she replied, eager to get started.

"This trip we're going my style." He indicated the ATV on the trailer. "I'm feeling a need to correct a bad rap. Not all ATV riders are ecological knuckle-draggers."

"Then I'll have to see if Red can keep an eye on the boys."

"Already taken care of."

"What about Rory?"

"Geneva's staying with him." He grinned. "Hey, your father's not the only one who can make things happen."

She couldn't help herself. She jumped him.

Threw her arms around his neck, her legs around his waist and kissed him full on the mouth. And he responded not like a sheriff, but like a man on twenty-four-hour leave. Boy, he could kiss!

When they drew apart they were both breathing

heavily. "This kind of behavior," he said, cocking one eyebrow, "is not going to get us very far up the trail."

"Let's go," she replied. "I want to leave civilization behind."

He quickly removed the ATV from its trailer. A narrow shelf on the back contained a cooler and his personal gear. He secured her stuff, then straddled the seat. "Hop on." He nodded over his shoulder.

She slid behind him and soon discovered it was far more agreeable to nestle up close to him than to sit back against the cooler.

As the late afternoon sun began to sink into the west, they took off east toward the Stones' farm until they came to a dirt track that ran between the two properties. "This is the old logging road," he said, letting the ATV engine idle. "It'll take us almost the whole way to the cabin."

"When was the property logged?"

"I'd say in Red's father's day."

"It makes me sad. To think of all those indigenous hardwoods harvested. Some, like the American chestnut, almost to extinction."

"Hey, I bet a few of those very hardwoods ended up in five-star hotels. Supply and demand, your father would say."

She should have been ticked at his comment, but he spoke the truth. And she'd been part of that truth, seeking out the best, the most exotic or simply the loveliest to complete the Singapore Ashley. She hadn't worried where her materials came from as long as the source didn't dry up.

He drove carefully, stopping often to point things out on the way. A family of deer grazing in a clearing. A particularly spectacular mass of mountain laurels. A pileated woodpecker, looking for all the world like a pterodactyl. She couldn't get over the fact that he was doing this for her.

Garrett thought he could easily get used to the sensation of Samantha up against him. This was the woman he was drawn to. Not the socialite or the high-powered businesswoman, who could probably buy and sell all of Applegate, but the wide-eyed llama farmer drawn to nature's every living thing. He might have been crazy to suggest this overnight trip, but he was tired of holding in and holding back. He couldn't tell what the morning might bring, but for now he was going to enjoy her warmth and her closeness.

Even though night was hours away, the sun had disappeared behind the treetops when they came to the end of the logging road and reached an ugly slash of land up against a ridge that had been stripped of its lumber years ago. Runoff and erosion had left little soil, and what was left supported a low growing scrub.

Garrett turned off the ATV's engine and pointed

to a gap through the ridge. "We hike through there to the cabin. It's not far."

He felt her shiver. "I hope it's prettier than this."

"It is. Because they couldn't get the big equipment through the gap, the forest hasn't been touched on the other side."

He shouldered his gear, then helped her with hers. Together they carried the cooler between them. It wasn't particularly heavy, but Garrett felt the weight of years of managing alone, of being in control, slip away with the simple shared task. How much of his isolation, he had to wonder, had been of his own doing?

When they reached the rustic one-room cabin, snug in the hollow amid old-growth trees like something out of "Hansel and Gretel," he was pleased to see that Rory and Red had done a little cleaning while they'd been stranded. It wasn't an Ashley International hotel, but the floor had been swept and the stone fireplace had freshly chopped wood stacked next to it. There was no furniture—the place had been built merely as a place for hunters to get out of the elements—but for an overnight stay he and Samantha wouldn't need anything more than they'd carried in.

"So what do you think of your cabin?" he asked, lowering his side of the cooler and slipping off his gear.

Her eyes wide and her smile luminous, she stood

in the middle of the room, turning slowly and looking up at the open beamwork. "It's absolutely wonderful. If I'd known this was here, I would have headed for the hills the minute I saw the limo coming up the county highway."

"Well, now you know. Of course, if you were to use this as a trek destination, you might have to reroute it to avoid that unsightly mess of scrub back there."

"I'm not going to use this for the treks." She ran her hand over the large, rough stones of the fireplace. "This is going to be my secret place."

"So you're saying you're gonna have to kill me."

She laughed, and the sound brightened the room. "Oh, no. For what I have in mind, I need you alive."

He liked the way this place made her bold. "What do you have in mind?" He placed his hand over hers on the stonework and leaned in.

Her mouth was barely an inch from his. "It's going to be cold tonight," she breathed, making him hot. "Surely this isn't enough wood to keep us warm. I'm going to need you to…chop more." Like a forest sprite, she ducked under his arm and ran out the door to dance around the cabin, singing, "Mine, mine, all of it mine!"

He leaned against the door frame and watched her until he was conscious his cheeks ached from smiling. "Come on!" he called. "If you like your cabin, you're going to love the spring."

"Spring?" she shouted, standing suddenly still, her hair in wild blond curls about her head. "I have my own spring?"

He held out his hand and when she took it, he led her farther into the hollow to an escarpment hung with vines. Out of a crevice flowed a small but steady, clear stream that tumbled down the rock face and disappeared in the thick, spongy moss beneath. He hadn't visited this place in years, but just hearing the gentle splashing, he could taste the cool, mineral water of his childhood summers with Mack. Like Samantha, he'd felt the healing magic of this place.

"Can I drink from it?" she asked when she saw the old wooden dipper hanging from a branch near the springhead.

"Sure, but it's not your ordinary supermarket bottled water taste."

Filling the dipper, she closed her eyes, then sipped as if she were some wine connoisseur. "Mmm. It's very cold. And tastes like…thunder and lightning."

He laughed. "I can't picture you in a business suit. What's the opposite of buttoned-down? Poetic?"

"That's a beautiful thing to say." She held out the dipper for him to drink. "I do feel freer because of this place. So far away from everyday pressures and expectations. And because of you…because you understood I needed to be brought here."

"I needed to bring you here." With this gentle woman, in this special place, he might be able to unravel the small, yet painful knot he'd carried around inside him his whole life. A daunting task.

"Funny, I don't think of you as having needs," she replied. "You're so in control."

"It's getting cool." He suddenly wondered if letting down his guard was such a good idea. "Let's gather up some more firewood and I'll try to explain while we make supper."

As Samantha picked up fallen tree branches on the way back to the cabin, she watched Garrett. What had he almost told her? And why had he stopped?

Ever since she'd moved to Applegate, she hadn't run into one person who had a bad word to say about the sheriff. She got the feeling he was a homegrown success story. In a few of them—Rachel, Red, Mack—she'd sensed a rather fierce protectiveness, yet for the life of her, she couldn't imagine a person less vulnerable than Garrett McQuire.

"You know you actually have to put the wood in the fireplace." Garrett's voice startled her.

She came out of her thoughts to see him standing in the cabin doorway. Tanned. Well muscled. Rugged. Framed and ready to be hung inside her locker door.

"Wh-what's for supper?" she asked.

"The one other meal I'm famous for besides trout. Beans and franks."

"Can we skewer the hot dogs on sticks and roast them over the fire?"

"So you want the gourmet version?"

"Absolutely."

"Then you're going to have to work for it." He reached out for the wood she carried. "I'll start the fire. You cut a couple switches to roast the franks."

"Did you bring a jackknife?"

He turned one hip to her. "In my pocket."

She hesitated and felt her cheeks grow hot.

"You afraid I'll bite?" he asked, his eyes full of an unexpected mischief.

Slowly she slid her hand into his pocket warmed by his body. As she grasped the knife, he leaned over and captured her earlobe with his teeth. The sensation was of being caught in some exquisite trap. Almost immediately he released her, but more than her ear had begun to tingle.

"I-I'd better put on my sweatshirt before I get those switches," she said, feeling as if they should be shedding clothes instead of adding more.

"Don't take too long. I'm hungry."

And so was she. In more ways than one. Wriggling into her sweatshirt, she dashed outside to cut two long, slender branches. She pared away the leaves and whittled the ends to sharp points, then hopped joyously back up the steps and into the cabin. The fire crackled, and beans already simmered in a pot hung on an iron hook embedded in the masonry. Garrett was spreading the sleeping bags on the floor in front of the fire. Not two separate sleeping bags, but each single opened then zippered together to form a double.

He looked up as she came in. "You did know we were headed here from the first day we met."

"Yes." Dismissing the prospect of food, she came to him and offered up her kisses.

And there, as the twilight gathered around the cabin and the birds sang a benediction, Samantha and Garrett made love. Not roughly or heedlessly, but tenderly as if they'd each been waiting for this moment for a very long time. As if they knew that what they shared was fragile and perhaps fleeting. Afterward, she lay in the crook of his arm, her cheek on his chest, listening to his heartbeat.

"Was this what you needed to bring me up here for?" she whispered.

"I'd be a liar if I said this wasn't part of it." He pulled the sleeping bag more closely about her shoulders. Wrapped both his arms around her. Kissed her hair. "But I also needed to see how you fit in a place that gave me—how can I explain it?—comfort as a kid."

She raised up on one elbow to look at his face. "What do you mean?"

"I know Red's told you I was in foster care. And maybe Mack's explained how he befriended me in grade school. How we roamed these hills. Here, I wasn't the outsider, the kid without a family. I just was. Although I don't think I can really explain it."

"You don't have to." She kissed the corner of his mouth and felt the sting of tears in her eyes. "I understand."

"I gave up camping and hunting when I got married. Noelle hated it, and I guess I figured the real me should be defined by family, not some forest."

"But when your marriage broke up, you felt as if you'd lost some innate part of you."

"Yeah." His eyebrows knit together in obvious pain. "Exactly."

"You didn't think of getting away occasionally with Mack?"

"No. We weren't kids anymore. Besides, Mack had gotten involved in the reserves. I just thought I needed to suck it up and move on."

"We all need someplace to step outside the role we've chosen. Or are forced to play." She grew wistful. "So, did I pass your test?"

"My test?"

"To see if I fit."

He pulled her down on top of him. "*We* fit," he declared huskily before making love to her again.

CHAPTER SEVENTEEN

AS THE MORNING SUN CUT ACROSS the cabin floor and he made coffee, fried bacon and eggs, Garrett couldn't take his eyes off the woman sleeping peacefully but a few feet away. Her hair spread out about her face like a wild, rippling current, her arm was flung above her head, and her mouth curved in a mysterious smile.

There was no mystery about the way Samantha made him feel. Alive. Whole. It's as if she'd poured balm on his unsettled soul.

Slowly, sensuously, she opened her eyes. "Good morning." Those might be his two, new favorite words in the English language. "I'm ravenous."

"You mean beans and franks at midnight weren't enough to tide you over?"

She stretched luxuriously. "I think we burned those calories and then some."

"Breakfast is almost ready. The restroom is—"

"I've been camping before," she said, crawling

out of the sleeping bag with a wink and nothing else. She rose, then, flashing him a grin over her shoulder, padded outside. As natural as the day she was born.

Garrett dropped the skillet on the stone hearth with a clatter. If she didn't watch it, they'd be eating breakfast—cold eggs and bacon—at noon.

When she returned, she pulled on shorts and a T-shirt as he dished out their meal. Lord, he was going to need the strength only protein could provide.

As she ate, she grew serious. "Considering how you were raised, you must hate Rory's custody arrangement."

"I do. It's no life being shuttled between parents."

"For you," she amended. "I think Rory's one of the most well-adjusted kids I've ever met."

Damn. She might be right. Yet he'd never until now uncoupled his own experience from that of his son.

"I still hate to think of him in London."

"Why?" She turned her soft hazel gaze on him. "There are daily trans-Atlantic flights."

"And phones. And e-mail. I know. You sound like Noelle."

"Don't make that a bad thing. Remember, she's half of what produced your well-adjusted kid."

He stole a strip of her bacon. "What makes you so charitable this morning?"

"This place. You. Really terrific sex." As he was

putting the bacon in his mouth, she leaned forward and caught the other end between her teeth and nibbled her way up to his lips. Her kiss lent new meaning to the phrase *honey-smoked.*

Needless to say, they didn't start back for Whistling Meadows until late morning.

HER ARMS WRAPPED AROUND Garrett's waist as they drove down the dirt track bordering the Stones' farm, Samantha noticed some unusual activity in the distance on the county road. Several vans with what looked like television satellite dishes were parked close to the ditch.

"No!" she breathed. Please, say they hadn't found her.

Garrett stopped the ATV and pulled out his cell phone. From the one-sided conversation, she understood he'd called headquarters. When he signed off, his expression was grim. "I'm going to cut across your property here," he said without further explanation.

"Is it…an accident?" She knew it wasn't.

"You could say that." In an instant, Garrett, the man, was gone. The sheriff was back. "We need to get you in the farmhouse."

She didn't like the sound of this.

When they drove into the barnyard, he pulled not in front near the cruiser and ATV trailer but up to the back steps. As soon as they'd stopped, he took her hand and quickly led her to the house, taking the keys from her to unlock the door. "Where's your TV?"

"In my bedroom."

He took the stairs two at a time. When she entered her room, he'd tuned the television to CNN. A talking head droned on about breaking news. She only half listened as she focused on Garrett staring at the screen. "Runaway heiress…rehab treatment for alcohol abuse…tiny hamlet in western North Carolina…"

Her photo flashed on the screen.

Her photo.

Oh. My. God.

She ran to the window and parted the blinds. Way down near the road a sheriff's department cruiser blocked the end of her drive. Standing next to the cruiser with shotguns cradled in their arms were two figures who could only be Mack and Red, keeping a crowd of a dozen or so reporters and cameramen at bay.

Her throat dry, her palms sweating, she whirled around to confront Garrett. "What the hell makes me newsworthy? I have never been able to figure that one out." She began to pace until Garrett reached out a hand to stop her.

His eyes were not unkind. "People crave stories about the rich and—"

"I wasn't some party girl courting celebrity," she

snapped. "My family's rich, yes. But we're hard-working rich. My grandfather was a shoe salesman. My father's a self-made man. I worked my ass off. Apparently so that some couch potato can get a smug sense of superiority when I take a nosedive."

He tried to take her in his arms, but she pushed him away. "Who would out me?"

"It damn well wasn't me," he said between clenched teeth as he shut off the television. "But, believe me, I'll find out who it was."

"Why would *I* be news?" she asked again, slumping onto the bed.

"Why ask why? This is the age of infotainment. A tabloid mentality. Insatiable, inappropriate curiosity. Reality shows where, at the same time, the grass is always greener and, as you said, someone else's troubles make the viewer feel better. It's sick, and I'm sick you're the object of it all right now."

"What am I going to do?"

"Nothing. You're going to stay here." He pulled out his phone again.

"Who are you calling?"

"Geneva. She'll stay with you."

His real meaning began to dawn on her. "I don't need *watching*."

"No. You need someone you can trust."

"What about you?"

"I have to get back to work. I have a feeling this county's going to heat up before it cools down. I'll stay till Geneva gets here. Why don't you take a shower. I'll be downstairs."

She went into the bathroom, closed the door, sat on the edge of the tub and called her mother.

"You can't believe what's happening," she said when Helena picked up.

"I can. I'm watching the news right now. An abomination. The Prescotts called to alert us as we were driving home. Which is where you should be. Home. Here. Where we have adequate staff to shield you. Your father will send the jet."

It was so tempting.

"No. This can't be more than a twenty-four-hour story. I'm going to ride it out on the farm."

"Darling, you're underestimating the interest. First you ran—"

"I did not *run*."

"Oh, let's not quibble. Appearance is everything." Her mother's voice had gone sharp. "Then you changed your name. The ratings chasers are going to think that's just the tip of the iceberg. They're going to keep digging. We need to present a united front as a family. If necessary we'll issue a press statement. Thank goodness Ashley International isn't a publicly traded company."

Appearances. The business. Samantha had had enough.

"Mother, don't you think you and Dad had something to do with all this?"

"What can you possibly mean?"

"You sweep into town in a limo—you couldn't have rented a Kia? Then you organize a very public, very extravagant, twenty-four-hour farmhouse make-over while Dad buys out my neighbor to keep me insulated from the locals. I came here to *quietly* recuperate while *fitting in.*"

"You make us sound so…forcefully subversive."

"Well?"

"Darling, calm down. How this disaster came about is not the issue. Right now you need us."

No. In coming to Applegate, Samantha had deliberately struck out on her own. If she wanted to prove her mettle, she needed to face this situation without her family's influence.

"Mother, I'm hanging up." And she did.

Which didn't make her feel any better.

By the time she'd showered and headed downstairs to make herself a cup of tea, Geneva had arrived and Garrett had left. Mack and Red were still guarding the head of her drive, making Samantha think she'd traded the Virginia solution for a modified North Carolina one.

She felt like a hostage.

GARRETT STARED OUT HIS OFFICE window onto Main Street. "The vultures," as he now referred to the reporters and their crew, were highly visible, although in the past three days most of the residents had refused to give interviews. Bless their hearts, as Mack's mother, Lily Whittaker, would say. "The vultures" were subsequently left interviewing "the gawkers"—folks who'd made Applegate a day-trip destination just to be part of the feeding frenzy. It was amazing how people, when confronted with a mike and a camera, could make jerks of themselves on a subject about which they knew absolutely nothing.

His cell phone rang. It was Noelle. He didn't pick up. He'd found out that, a few days back, she'd phoned a cousin in Asheville to ask if she knew anything about the possibility that the Lawrences of Ashley International Hotels were vacationing in Applegate, of all places. The cousin had called an aunt who'd called a friend who just happened to be the editor for the *Western Carolina Sun* "Living" section, and the rest was history. Which—although it would be convenient to blame his ex—made Garrett the source of the leak. Stemming from the one phone call he hadn't stopped himself from making. He'd lost his right to pass judgment on other people's insatiable curiosity.

Now, of course, Noelle didn't want Rory in the middle of the mess. Samantha had emphatically agreed. So Rory was running errands in town for the department and getting updates from Geneva, Red and Mack. Samantha had also insisted Garrett not put a deputy on her property. She didn't want any hint of preferential treatment. He'd complied but made sure his staff continuously cruised that strip of county road. He'd only talked to her once since they'd returned from the cabin but hadn't seen her.

He missed her.

Rory walked into the office. "Rachel needs you over at the diner."

"Did she say what it's about?"

Rory shook his head. "I gotta run an errand for Red. He wants me to see if the hardware store has two dozen No Trespassing signs. If they do, I'm supposed to put it on the Whistling Meadows tab. Then can I deliver them?"

"No. I'll have one of the deputies drop them off."

"Dad…are you mad at Samantha?"

"Why would you ask that?"

"You haven't gone to the farm. You won't let me see her."

"I'm just trying to cut down on the speculation. The media watches everyone who goes in and comes out of Whistling Meadows." In fact, a photo taken with a powerful telephoto lens of Garrett and Samantha on the ATV had turned up in a national tabloid with the headline, The Sheriff and the Social-ite and the subheading, Love Nest Uncovered.

"But you seem upset," Rory persisted.

He was. At himself.

"'Cause she's not the person you thought she was?"

Apparently, in prying into her private life, *he* wasn't the person he'd thought he was.

"I know you don't like liars…" Rory screwed up his face as if trying to find the right words. "But if this is the kind of stuff she faced back in her old life, maybe she thought the only way to escape was to start all over again. With a new name and everything."

Sadly, if she'd done it once when the going got tough, she could do it again.

"Dad?"

Garrett slipped his arm around his son's shoulders. "All that's water under the bridge. Right now, my job's to make sure no one gets hurt. You included."

Rory looked at him as if he expected more.

"I need to find out what Rachel wants, and you need to check on those signs."

Outside on the sidewalk someone stuck a mike in his face. "Sheriff McQuire! What is your explanation of the photo circulating in the tabloids?"

"No comment."

"Do you think the voters of Colum County will see this as an issue come the next election?"

He didn't even rise to that one.

At the diner he plowed through reporters waiting for cameramen, and cameramen waiting for reporters on the steps outside. Rachel would serve the media, but she wouldn't allow their equipment in her establishment, creating a tag team approach to eating. All heads turned as Garrett stepped through the doorway, but Rachel immediately intercepted him.

"I need to speak to you in private," she said, leading him through the kitchen and into the very back of the diner. Abruptly, she shoved him into the storeroom, then closed the door behind him. Standing in the dim light of a single overhead bulb was Samantha. Dressed in Geneva's clothes, which were way too big for her, she looked tired.

"How did you get here?" he asked.

"I cut across the outer pasture to the Stones' farm. Isolde brought me in."

He thought of "the vultures" just outside. "You want me to take you back to Whistling Meadows, is that it?"

"No. I'm not going back to Whistling Meadows. Geneva's daughter's coming for me in a half hour. She's going to drive me to Atlanta."

The painful inner knot that had started to unravel up at the cabin began to tighten around his heart.

"Who's going to take care of your llamas? The farm?"

"Red and Mack."

"Where are you going from Atlanta?"

She sighed. "I don't know yet."

"If you knew, would you tell me?"

"No. Then you'd have to lie for me."

He stepped forward to take her in his arms, but she put up her hand. "I'm sorry," she said.

"How long will you be gone?"

"I don't know that, either. At least as long as it takes for the media to clear out of Applegate. I thought the furor would have died down by now, but since it hasn't, it's not fair of me to disrupt people's lives here."

"Maybe we needed to have our lives disrupted."

She didn't answer.

"When you come back, will you stay?"

"I don't know." She moved past him toward the door. "I just wanted to say goodbye."

"That's it, then?"

"Yes." She reached for the doorknob, but he grasped her wrist.

"Stay and show your true colors, Samantha. You know who you are. Who you want to be. People in town are standing firm behind you."

"I'm afraid if this circus doesn't move on, they'll quickly lose their stomach for the drama."

"Don't underestimate them. Or yourself. All you have to do to prove yourself a bona fide Applegate citizen is to plant your feet on Whistling Meadows and refuse to leave."

"It's not that easy." There was anguish in her eyes.

"Because you never meant to stay," he said bitterly. Catching on.

"I—I wanted to. But I didn't know if I could."

"What kind of an answer is that?"

"The only one I have. I was vulnerable when I arrived. I couldn't guess what role the town, the farm, the people would play in my recovery. I didn't know how strong I'd be."

"You have to tell me," he said. "What role did I play?"

"You're angry—"

"You're damned right I'm angry. Because you're blowing everything off. Blowing me off."

She put her fingers on his lips. "Don't say something you'll regret."

He thought about how he'd opened up to her overnight at the cabin. Physically and emotionally. He certainly regretted that, big-time.

Rachel poked her head into the room. "Geneva's daughter's here."

And just like that, Samantha slipped out of his life.

CHAPTER EIGHTEEN

FOR THE FIRST WEEK AFTER Samantha left town, Garrett kept busy controlling the dwindling media horde. It actually took a couple days before "the vultures" realized their prey had escaped. And two days after that, "the gawkers" moved on to the next breaking story.

And then Applegate returned to normal. At least everybody else seemed to breathe a sigh and settle back into their pre-media-blitz existence. Garrett felt as if he was coming down with the flu.

During the second week, Rory begged to help Red up at Whistling Meadows. Red assured Garrett Rory would get paid. Samantha had given him the power to hire and reimburse any help he might need maintaining the llamas and the farm. Mack was already working there, which irked Garrett not a little as he was short staffed, yet he'd kept Mack's deputy position unfilled.

In the end, Rory rode his bike to the farm while

Garrett avoided the stretch of two-lane running by Samantha's property.

After three weeks had gone by, people started approaching Garrett with blind date offers. Oh, in true Applegate fashion, they didn't discuss what they did or didn't know about him and Samantha. And they didn't come right out and say they were trying to fix him up. They just innocently happened to mention that their daughter, granddaughter, cousin once removed, or friend of a friend was going to be in town and they were having a little get-together. Would Garrett like to join them?

He wouldn't, and he didn't.

He was still angry with Samantha for leaving. And still angry with himself for exposing her and forcing her to go.

He hadn't heard from her.

When almost a month had gone by, Jonathan Stone took a seat at the counter next to Garrett in the diner. "Can I have a word with you, Sheriff?"

"That depends. If your single great-niece is in town visiting, this conversation's over."

"Tetchy." Jonathan grinned. "But considering my track record—" he'd been married three times "—I'd be the last person to dabble in matchmaking. No, I'm here in my capacity as selectman. We've set a date for the road bowling tournament. Second Saturday in August. The ninth. That'll give you two weeks to put the road-closing signs up."

"What route will you be using?"

"Red Harris suggested we start at the top of the old dirt logging track that runs between Whistling Meadows and my place, then onto the paved county highway and right down into Main Street."

"We're talking a pretty steep grade."

"That's what'll make it interesting."

"How many people participating?"

"Seeing how it's our first year, we cut registration off at twenty teams. Plus, each team will have an impartial scorekeeper drawn on the morning of the tournament."

"Sixty crazy people let loose on county roads." Garrett turned back to his coffee. "I can't wait."

Rachel came over and plunked a slice of cherry pie with vanilla ice cream in front of Garrett. "On the house. Seems you could use a little sugar, Sheriff."

He was fine. He just needed to find that equilibrium, that emotional autopilot he'd been cruising on before Samantha had hit town.

"Hey, Dad!" Rory came through the door. His hair was sun-streaked and tousled and his tanned arms were beginning to show some muscle. "Mom here yet?"

"She said suppertime." Garrett checked his watch. "It's only one o'clock." Noelle had finally agreed to a face-to-face meeting to discuss the custody arrangement. He'd put the fire department on alert. "What are you doing in town? I thought you were working until four."

"I am," Rory replied between mouthfuls of cherry pie he was cadging from Garrett's plate. "I'm in town to get yard sale signs."

"For whom?"

"Red." His son scowled. "He got a letter this morning from Samantha, telling him to sell everything in the house."

The statement hit like a thunderclap. "Is she selling Whistling Meadows?"

"She didn't say."

Surely the sale of the farmhouse contents was a first step. Why, after a month, did the news cut so deep?

"Dad, I know you told me to leave this whole Samantha and the media thing to the adults, but…I gotta say, you need to talk to Red. Get Samantha's address or phone number or something. Convince her she can't just up and leave Applegate. The llamas. Us."

How could he? Seemed she'd already made up her mind.

"I know you'll do the right thing," Rory said, crimson pie filling streaking his mouth. "Gotta run. I'm excited to see Mom."

Garrett felt as if he'd been blindsided, but why

should he? Samantha had held out no hope that she'd be back. He'd made her no promises, and neither had she. Although, since her flight from Applegate, she hadn't shown up on the news—yeah, he'd watched for her—and since he had no idea where she was, he pictured her back in her old lifestyle. He didn't exactly know what that might involve—except money—however, he'd bet that the Lawrences weren't road bowling.

To the obvious dismay of his staff, he pretty much growled his way through the rest of the afternoon. He couldn't help himself. By the time Noelle's Lexus pulled into his driveway, he was a walking headache.

"Pull yourself together for Rory," Geneva said as Garrett stood in his living room and glared out the front window at his ex getting out of her luxury car. His housekeeper was putting on her cardigan.

"You aren't leaving, are you?"

"Y'all agreed on pizza. You don't need me." She glanced behind him. "How you doin', Noelle?"

He turned to see her standing in the doorway. She was still in a business suit. "Geneva. Garrett."

"Rory's in his room," Geneva said as she left. "He's got those earbuds in, so you're gonna hafta holler at him."

When it was just the two of them, Noelle looked as uncomfortable as Garrett felt. Ever since the chain of events that had caused such an uproar in Apple-gate, she'd been remarkably subdued. "Maybe we should take this opportunity to talk."

"About custody? I don't think so. Rory wants to be here for that discussion. In fact, I think he's put together a PowerPoint presentation to support his case."

She actually smiled. "His e-mails come close to a campaign. He doesn't just tell me what he's doing. He frames everything in college-course terms. Feeding the llamas is animal husbandry. Building a fence is applied trig. Managing his paycheck is finance one-o-one."

"That's our boy." Suddenly, he thought of Samantha encouraging him to speak positively of Noelle because she was the other half of the equation that had contributed to the good kid Rory was. "You've done a great job raising him."

She looked surprised. "Wh-why, thank you."

"You want some of Geneva's peach tea?"

"That would be nice." She followed him into the kitchen. "Actually, I wanted to talk to you about something other than custody. I wanted to say I'm sorry I caused such trouble for your girlfriend."

He stood with the fridge door open. "My girlfriend?"

"Yes. Ashley Lawrence. Or Samantha Weston. Anyway, I called my cousin for no reason other than I was beside myself with curiosity. It was very unprofessional."

"Samantha's not my girlfriend."

"That's not what Rory says."

"What does Rory say?"

"He says he thinks the only thing keeping her from coming back is that you haven't told her how you feel."

"I don't know how she feels."

"Oh, I think you do." She took the pitcher of iced tea from the refrigerator and poured three glasses. "Garrett, women don't like to be kept guessing. We like to be told."

"Funny, I remember I told you I wanted to stay in Applegate, and you told me to get lost."

"That was different. This woman actually loves Applegate."

"It's not that easy. What would keep the media away if she came back?"

"Oh, I don't know. Maybe a few diehards would hang around for a while. The locals already seem to have a pretty good handle on ignoring them. But if Samantha were to, say, return to the farm, settle down, have a steady boyfriend, get married, lead an ordinary life…well, inquiring minds would eventually say, 'Hey, that sounds an awful lot like my day-to-day,' and turn away to find a more titillating subject—"

"Mom!" Rory burst into the room to envelope his mother in a hug that lifted her right off the floor. For

the first time Garrett noticed how much their son—
and his ex—had grown over the summer.

NERVOUS, SAMANTHA PACED THE hallway outside the
sheriff's office and tried to ignore the stares of the
deputies. After more than four weeks away from Applegate, she had no idea what faced her. She told
herself to have no expectations. Garrett hadn't said
he'd wait for her. In fact, when she'd left Rachel's
storeroom, he'd looked justifiably angry.

She chewed on a knuckle and waited for Mack to
finish his business beyond Garrett's closed office door.
While he'd given her a ride from the farm, Mack had
told her it was time for him to stop hiding out. Time
to step up and take responsibility again. There was
something stark in his eyes when he'd said it, as though
resuming his duties as deputy was a penance. Or
maybe she was reading too much into it. Maybe he was
cautioning her to step up and take responsibility, too.

She was going to give it a shot.

The office door opened.

Mack appeared but paused, then turned to speak
over his shoulder. "By the way, there's someone I'd
like you to meet. She's new in town—"

"Not you, too!" Garrett's voice sounded like the
roar of a bear in its lair. "I've had it with match-
makers."

"Don't insult the woman before you check her out. She's right here." Mack pulled her into the office. "Garrett McQuire meet Samantha Weston. I believe that's your legal name now, isn't it?"

"Y-yes." The word stuck in her throat as Garrett rose from behind his desk to confront her, his brow furrowed, his blue eyes almost indigo, revealing nothing.

She didn't hear Mack leave, but when she finally came to her senses, Garrett and she were alone, the office door closed.

His stance stiff, he looked as if he didn't have a clue what to say to her. "When did you get back?" he asked finally.

"Early this morning. Red picked me up at the airport."

"I suppose you wanted to be here to supervise the big yard sale tomorrow."

"Red, Rory and Mack could have handled it. But, yes, I admit I wanted to see all that stuff leave. It wasn't me."

"So you decided you really were Samantha Weston."

"I am. Although it took a rather noisy family intervention—refereed by Dr. Kumar—to make my parents see I wasn't just hiding out. Wasn't using a temporary alias the way celebrities do when they check into our hotels."

He came around the desk to sit on the corner. He didn't offer her a seat. He seemed to be waiting for some kind of opening. Or a sign. "You went home, then."

"I couldn't go back to Virginia because the media had camped outside my parents' estate. We all met up at the Fiji Ashley. I then used that as my base camp."

"Good move," he noted dryly. "A slob with a reporter's salary probably couldn't afford the airfare."

She ignored the dig. "Anyway, when I'd taken care of business, I came back to Applegate. So, tell me, did you reach a new custody agreement with Noelle?"

He appeared to soften with this new tack. "Yeah. Surprisingly, we did."

"Why do you say *surprisingly?*"

"I tried to concentrate on something…a friend said. I tried to let go of my anger and frustration in dealing with Noelle—the fact that my ego had been bruised big-time when she left, when she proved she could be just as good a provider as me—and concentrate on the positive. Rory. How he loves us both."

Her heart went out to him, and a smile just naturally curved her lips. "And how did that work out?"

"Noelle's a good mother. She wants what's best for Rory. So I sat back and let Rory convince her he'd love to see England—on his vacations—but that Applegate is who he is."

"I understand exactly how he feels."

"You do?" For the first time there was hope in Garrett's eyes. "Then…you're not just back in town to oversee the yard sale?"

"Gosh, no. Mack signed us up for the road bowling tournament next week. With Rory and Red making up another team, Whistling Meadows has a pretty good chance at the trophy. And the boys haven't been on a decent trek since I left. Red has spoiled them rotten. Percy fairly lives in the bunkhouse."

A wide grin split his handsome features. "You're really staying?"

"I'm back. For good. But you didn't give me a chance to tell you the biggest reason."

"Which is?" He stood and took a step closer.

Her heart beat so fast her hands shook. "I missed trout for breakfast."

He scooped her into his arms and spun her around. "Damn, I love you."

"You do? You could have told me."

Letting her gently down to the floor, he nuzzled her neck. "I was stupid. I let the past eat at me. I kept asking myself what I could offer you."

"*You,* silly. Openly. Honestly. Just the way you did up at the cabin."

"Well, then you've got me. And the cabin. And an occasional Motel 6 if we venture out of Applegate."

"I draw the line there, buster," she replied, laughing. "I may be out of the hotel business, but I think we can do better than that."

He kissed her hard and fast and deep, and all she could think of as her head spun was, *This is right where I'm supposed to be.*

EPILOGUE

Four months later

GARRETT, SAMANTHA AND RORY stood in the international concourse of the Atlanta airport as Rory was about to board his flight for London and his Christmas vacation with Noelle. Having lived with his son every day since the beginning of summer, Garrett was having difficulty letting him go for two weeks. Had Noelle felt this wrenching pain each vacation when the custody arrangement had been reversed? He felt new admiration for her strength.

As if she understood his inner turmoil, Samantha slipped her hand in his and squeezed. He shouldn't be surprised. This amazing woman was like a part of him.

"You'd better get on the plane," Garrett said to Rory, unable to eliminate the catch in his voice. "Do you have everything you need?"

"I'd better." Rory stared directly at Garrett. "Do *you* have everything?"

"Yes." He could feel the small box resting in his jacket's inner pocket.

"I could stay a few minutes more." His son looked behind him to the gate where people were already boarding. "If you need help."

"Some things a man has to do by himself, kid."

"What are you two talking about?" Samantha asked.

"Nothing!" Rory tried for the innocent look— he'd make a horrible poker player. "See y'all after the New Year," he said, waving goodbye and trotting over to the diminishing line of passengers.

"Don't forget to e-mail!" Garrett called out.

They stayed until the plane took off. As soon as it was out of sight, he turned to Samantha. She had tears in her eyes.

"I'm okay. I'm okay," she said, swiping at her face. "I just get a little sentimental at the holidays."

"Then maybe you need an early present."

"I don't need any presents. I have you," she said as she stepped so close there was nothing between them. Nothing but happiness and a sense of wholeness. "Have I told you lately that I love you?"

"You have, but I never get tired of hearing it." He kissed her lightly on her nose, then pulled the jewelry box from his pocket. "Samantha Weston," he said, "I know you just went through a name change…but would you consider another? Or, at least, a hyphenated version?"

"What are you asking?"

He opened the box to reveal a platinum band set with four small diamonds. One for her. One for him. One for Rory. One for the future. "Will you marry me?"

"Of course I will!" she exclaimed and threw her arms around his neck to the applause of holiday travelers on the concourse.

"There's just one stipulation," he said.

She raised an eyebrow. "Stipulations already?"

"Rory says he's to be the best man. So the date has to coincide with his time with us."

"Hmm. How about spring break?"

"He'll be in—"

"London, yes. And the London Ashley is the Lawrence flagship hotel. I have an in."

"Your parents won't have the maid short the sheets?"

She laughed, and, as if to capture that laughter and feed his soaring spirits, he lowered his mouth to hers.

Bundles of Joy—
coming next month
to Superromance

Experience the romance, excitement and joy with 6 heartwarming titles.

BABY, I'M YOURS #1476 by *Carrie Weaver*

ANOTHER MAN'S BABY
(The Tulanes of Tennessee)
#1477 by *Kay Stockham*

THE MARINE'S BABY (9 Months Later)
#1478 by *Rogenna Brewer*

BE MY BABIES (Twins)
#1479 by *Kathryn Shay*

THE DIAPER DIARIES (Suddenly a Parent)
#1480 by *Abby Gaines*

HAVING JUSTIN'S BABY (A Little Secret)
#1481 by *Pamela Bauer*

Exciting, Emotional and Unexpected!

*Look for these Superromance titles in March 2008.
Available wherever books are sold.*

REQUEST YOUR FREE BOOKS!
2 FREE NOVELS PLUS 2 FREE GIFTS!

HARLEQUIN®

Super Romance®

Exciting, emotional, unexpected!

YES! Please send me 2 FREE Harlequin Superromance® novels and my 2 FREE gifts. After receiving them, if I don't wish to receive any more books, I can return the shipping statement marked "cancel." If I don't cancel, I will receive 6 brand-new novels every month and be billed just $4.69 per book in the U.S., or $5.24 per book in Canada, plus 25¢ shipping and handling per book and applicable taxes, if any*. That's a savings of close to 15% off the cover price! I understand that accepting the 2 free books and gifts places me under no obligation to buy anything. I can always return a shipment and cancel at any time. Even if I never buy another book from Harlequin, the two free books and gifts are mine to keep forever.

135 HDN EEX7 336 HDN EEYK

Name	(PLEASE PRINT)
Address	Apt.
City	State/Prov.	Zip/Postal Code

Signature (if under 18, a parent or guardian must sign)

Mail to the **Harlequin Reader Service**®:
IN U.S.A.: P.O. Box 1867, Buffalo, NY 14240-1867
IN CANADA: P.O. Box 609, Fort Erie, Ontario L2A 5X3

Not valid to current Harlequin Superromance subscribers.

Want to try two free books from another line?
Call 1-800-873-8635 or visit www.morefreebooks.com.

* Terms and prices subject to change without notice. NY residents add applicable sales tax. Canadian residents will be charged applicable provincial taxes and GST. This offer is limited to one order per household. All orders subject to approval. Credit or debit balances in a customer's account(s) may be offset by any other outstanding balance owed by or to the customer. Please allow 4 to 6 weeks for delivery.

Your Privacy: Harlequin is committed to protecting your privacy. Our Privacy Policy is available online at www.eHarlequin.com or upon request from the Reader Service. From time to time we make our lists of customers available to reputable firms who may have a product or service of interest to you. If you would prefer we not share your name and address, please check here. ☐

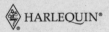

COMING NEXT MONTH

#1476 BABY, I'M YOURS · Carrie Weaver
As a recently widowed mom with three kids, Becca Smith struggles to keep life together. The discovery that she's pregnant is making things worse. There's only one person she can turn to—Rick Jensen. He's her business partner...and possibly this baby's father.

#1477 ANOTHER MAN'S BABY · Kay Stockham
The Tulanes of Tennessee
Landing in the ditch while in premature labor is not on Darcy Rhodes's to-do list. Fortunately, rescue arrives in the form of Garret Tulane. He seems so perfect, he's like Prince Charming. But will they forge their own happily ever after once the snow stops?

#1478 THE MARINE'S BABY · Rogenna Brewer
9 Months Later
Joining the military taught Lucky Calhoun the importance of family. And now he wants one of his own. That wish may come true sooner than planned. Thanks to a mix-up at the sperm bank, Caitlin Calhoun—his half brother's widow—seems to be carrying his child.

#1479 BE MY BABIES · Kathryn Shay
Twins
Simon McCarthy should not be attracted to Lily Wakefield. Not only is she new to town, but also she's pregnant—with twins. Still, the feelings between them make him think about their future together. Then her past catches up and threatens to destroy everything.

#1480 THE DIAPER DIARIES · Abby Gaines
Suddenly a Parent
A baby is so not playboy Tyler Warrington's thing. Still, he must care for the one who appeared on his doorstep. Fine. Hire a nanny. Then Bethany Hart talks her way into the job—for a cost. Funny, the more time he spends with her, the more willing he is to pay.

#1481 HAVING JUSTIN'S BABY · Pamela Bauer
Justin Collier has been Paige Stephens's best friend forever. Then one night she turns to him for comfort and...well, everything changes. Worse, she's now pregnant and he's proposing! She's always wanted to marry for love, but can Justin offer her that?